REBORN IN FLAMES

M. SINCLAIR

Copyright © M. Sinclair, 2019. All rights reserved.

No portion of this book may be reproduced in any form without permission from the publisher, except as permitted by U.S. copyright law. This book is a work of fiction and any resemblance to persons, living or dead, or places, events, or locales is purely coincidental. The characters are products of the author's imagination and used fictitiously.

Warnings: Please be advised that the book contains darker themes such as child abuse, PTSD, swearing, and violence. Additionally, sexual themes are suitable for mature audiences +18.

The Union of Love & Madness

CONTENTS

Description	vii
Prologue - Marco	1
1. Maya	5
2. Maya	23
3. Atlas	49
4. Maya	52
5. Henry	67
6. Maya	72
7. Sai	82
8. Maya	87
9. Ledger	98
10. Maya	104
11. Anani	117
12. Maya	121
13. Maya	132
14. Maya	151
15. Marco	154
16. Maya	160
17. Atlas	166
18. Maya	172
19. Henry	180
20. Maya	186
21. Sai	193
22. Maya	198
23. Croy	213
24. Maya	216
25. Ledger	228
Epilogue - Maya	232

Also by M. Sinclair   235
Following me: 237

DESCRIPTION

I have spent my entire life in the basement of my father's church. My sadistic mother and god-fearing father believe I have the devil inside me because I heal after their abuse. I'd accepted long ago I would die in the very place I'd been born without ever feeling the sun on my skin. Then one day, my mother took me from my father's religious cult in the wake of his death. Nearly a week later, and after countless hours with her boyfriend Jed's creepy remarks, I find myself in Washington State. I had only ever interacted with my parents and now Jed, so you can imagine my surprise when I ran smack dab into possibly the most handsome man in the world. He's not alone though, there are intriguing and handsome men popping up everywhere in my life.

Except I shouldn't be focusing on that. I should be preparing for my mother's cruel hits. Preparing to run the minute I turn 18. Preparing to hide from Jed's leering comments and uncomfortable stares. One interaction with this man and I feel like my entire life has been altered.

Five days until I turn 18. *Five days* until my mother realizes what happens when you keep a bird cooped up for too long, only to open its cage. *Five days* until I am out of here.

My problem? Everything inside of me tells me that those intriguing men are mine... and they seem to think the same.

This is a slow/medium burn fantasy RH that features a naive but strong MFC with a troubled past and a secret about what she really is. Come meet Maya and her protective and possessive dragon shifters! This book will be part of the **Reborn** series.

Warnings: Please be advised that the book contains darker themes such as child abuse, PTSD, swearing, and violence. Additionally, sexual themes are suitable for mature audiences +18. This book will end on a slight cliffhanger.

PROLOGUE - MARCO

We pulled into town and the faint scent of the shoreline assaulted my nose through the open window of the car. It brought a small smile to my face. *Home.* Not the home I'd been born in. Not the family I'd been born into. No, this was my home. A home that my flight and I had chosen for ourselves. Washington State. We lived in a small town that wasn't known for anything except the massive lighthouse it featured. It was why we loved it. After everything we've been through, we craved the peace and serenity it had to offer.

"Want anything from inside?" I asked Atlas. He grunted with a shake of his head before he closed his eyes once more. Our drive from Los Angeles had exhausted both of us and the reason for being there had left us both ready to sleep for the next week. I parked my BMW at the pump before standing up to go inside. My dress pants were wrinkled and my hair laid in a million different directions. What I needed right now? To get home and take a long fucking shower before passing out.

Did I need to emphasize anymore how much I needed sleep right now?

Instinctually, I categorized the one other car, a black rusted-out Ford, parked in front of the gas station shop. There was a larger woman inside in the passenger seat, but the windows were tinted, so I couldn't get a good look at her. Something about the car made me feel off. I put it from my thoughts as I entered the shop and crossed the broken tiled floor to pay for my tank of gas. Outside, the gloomy sky thundered as it began to spit out heavy rain.

I turned toward the bathroom and made my way down the aisle, only to be run into by a young boy. I grunted as the small frame collided with my chest and swayed on his feet. A hiss of pain came from the figure as I steadied him with a solid grip on his small arms.

"Sorry," the soft voice murmured quietly.

"No problem..." I stopped talking as my eyes widened. My hands tightened on the small frame as *her* hood came down. The person I'd thought a boy was, in fact, a young woman. My dragon hissed in recognition as a pair of soft brown eyes, speckled with gold, stared back at me.

I immediately picked up the scent of sea salt, ashes, and roses on her golden skin. It was obvious she wasn't human, but I couldn't for the life of me recognize her scent. Instead, I categorized every element of her soft, wavy chocolate hair that shimmered with gold streaks and fell to her waist once released from her hood. She had the tiniest button nose and thick dark lashes that fluttered nervously. It was possible that she was the most feminine woman I'd ever met. She was just so damn beautiful. Like a rose or something equally as beautiful.

Then I noticed the way her soft pink mouth twisted in pain. I loosened my tightening grip on her thin shoulders.

Why was she so thin? Did she need food? We could get her food. Also, a jacket. This wasn't heavy enough for how cold it was.

Fuck. My dragon was in a protective overdrive. This was bad.

"I need to go," she muttered, her voice raspy.

Was she sick? Why was no one taking care of her? If she wanted, I could take care of her. As in, she could come home with me to our flight house. Now. She would have literally anything she ever wanted. *And* I was going to lose my mind if I didn't learn this woman's name.

"Maya," a voice growled from behind her, "leave this man alone."

The woman shrunk down into herself, like a wilted flower. Her eyes took on a dull hue as a massive man, nearly matching Atlas' 6'5" height, appeared over her shoulder. He looked like a mean son of a bitch, but completely human. Those black eyes took note of my hands on Maya and a yellow-toothed sneer took over his face.

"Get in line buddy, she's a fucking tease," he chuckled, grabbing her hood in a taunting manner before pulling her toward the door.

I yanked her back to me, not caring about the obvious show of supernatural strength, wanting her against my chest. Safe there. My instincts were begging me to hide this woman from him. Maya. What a beautiful name. A worried whimper came from her throat as the man in front of us grew red in the face.

"It's fine," she mumbled softly before stepping out from behind my back.

Why was she resigned to his obvious disrespect? I didn't think this man was her father, but who was he then? Was this the person put in charge of watching her? I slipped a thin business card into her jogger pockets and realized she was even thinner than I'd assumed. God. I wanted to help her, but the look in her eyes told me it wasn't the time. No matter. I had her scent. I would find her.

"Come on little bitch, back to the car," the man snarled before herding her out the door. She looked back only once before offering me a barely-there smile. I felt my heart thump with deep low strums. My dragon roared aggressively in my head. He didn't care what she wanted or what the man wanted. He wanted her back here.

I didn't disagree.

"Who the hell was that?" Atlas' low baritone voice asked from the door. His eyes were filled with gold and the realization she had affected both of us had my mind working overtime.

The black truck squealed out of the gas station. I could see her faint outline from the back as the man in the front opened his mouth in what I assumed were screams. It didn't matter though, I would find her. I would help her.

"That is," I sighed as the distance grew and my heart squeezed uncomfortably, "our mate."

1
MAYA

I laughed at my father's death.
 That must mean my mother's right. *I do have the devil inside of me.* It didn't stop the unadulterated joy from slipping out. Of course, that was mixed with a sigh of disappointment because only the world could be so cruel. After all the years of torture I'd endured, he'd gotten a peaceful death in his sleep.

So I laughed. I never saw the body, but she'd told me in a rather dismissive tone while stating we were leaving. It was funny in sort of a sick, sad, way. Of course, the beating I'd received from my mother had been terrible, but that would have happened whether or not Pastor Malcolm had passed this previous May. She hadn't done it for any special occasion. She had handcrafted the oddball shape of abuse and ingenuousness that could be labeled 'Maya.'

Despite my very short time in real society, I had found a truth that seemed to hold true. Some people did not fit in. We were just different. The difference in how we viewed the world through our smudged, broken lenses, made us stand out and not in a good way.

These individuals did not belong in high school. Yet, here I was for the first time ever in my life. 5 days before my eighteenth birthday. I'd survived 17 years and 11 months of my life. On September 2nd, my new life would start. My new life away from her.

It seemed I'd be doing it here in Washington as well. My mother decided to move us across the country from my father's religious cult, to move in with Jed. I hated Jed. I really had no idea *what* I would do in 5 days, but I would rather be homeless than to live with my mother and Jed. After around a week of driving across the country, I had already grown tired of his antics and uncomfortable remarks. Plus, my mother grew angrier each and every time he focused on me. Before I'd left our trailer this morning to walk to school, she'd berated me with a belt until I had been left terribly bruised. Luckily, she hadn't broken skin. My new school uniform wouldn't have covered the blood.

I really did not belong here.

Yet, my sneakered feet still crossed the perfectly paved parking lot. You would have thought that my mother would be hesitant to let me wander the world by myself, but as she mentioned, it hadn't been her idea to keep me in the basement. She hadn't wanted me at all. No, the basement was all my father's idea. So why she kept me around now, I had no idea.

I shook the thoughts from my head.

The school was extravagant, to say the least. Then again, I had been homeschooled from the basement of my church. I had been *so thankful* Pastor Malcolm had read to me from scripture. I mean, what else would have distracted me from the beatings and pain. My eyes narrowed on the dark gothic stone and arched doorways. Every inch of the pavement crawled with expensive cars and beautifully pressed uniforms. I had no idea how my mother and Jed were sending me here. I lived in a trailer. My uniform didn't fit compared to the other students. The clothing items sure as hell weren't pressed. Honestly, the soft wrinkled material felt better on my bruised body.

I suddenly felt smaller than I ever had in my entire life. I stood around five and a half feet tall and was underfed. Malnourished. I wish I could have admitted to some trendy diet. Ha. I supposed if you counted 'fasting to rid the devil from your body' as a diet, I had been on one. No. The truth was far more depressing. I looked over the dark gray plaid skirt that hung off my hip bones and worn black hoodie that I hoped to get away with. Underneath, I had a white polo that had arrived in the mail with my complete uniform. It was the nicest piece of clothing I had ever owned. However, it showed off far too many bruises for my liking. I may not know a lot, but I did know bruises usually weren't viewed as a good thing. I curled my toes up inside my worn shoe. It was cold here, far colder than Louisiana had been.

I whimpered as my backpack hit against a part of my back that was bruised. This morning had been relatively easy in comparison to most. It still hurt though. Unfortunately, since she hadn't broken skin, my helpful healing ability hadn't kicked in. Bruises didn't count apparently.

The devil rights your body because of the sin inside you. The sin inside you.

I hadn't placed much thought into my healing ability, ever. Nor had I asked anyone about it. I had only ever interacted with Pastor Malcolm, my mother, and now Jed. They wouldn't tell me what they knew. Besides, I was far too busy surviving. I just knew that if blood was shed, my body would heal itself overnight. It was why my mother now tried to not spill blood. Instead, she bruised my body until it was unrecognizable in the mirror.

My thoughts strayed to the gas station yesterday. If that social interaction was anything to base the future from, I was nervous. I had never interacted with someone close to my age, so it had been a moment of revelation to me. And what a moment it had been. Like, holy cow.

His name was Marco, I think. His card was in my backpack. I didn't plan on calling him, didn't have a way to, but it made me feel safe to have him near me. Even in paper form. That was how Marco had made me feel. Safe.

It was clear he was a man of power. The way he stood, and how he dressed, it was obvious he was powerful and demanding. He had been tall, much taller than me, and dressed in expensive clothes. He would have fit in much better here than myself. I could still feel the way his warm hands had curled against my bruised arms. The action had bathed me in heat and security. I had lost all ability to articulate around him.

Did all men smell like vanilla and fresh snow? I knew those scents well. When Pastor Malcolm had left the basement window open, I could often smell the season change and scents from the church's kitchen above. I let my mind drift to the sharp, clean, cut of his tanned jaw and the way his dark hair seemed to lay in a styled mess. It was his pale green eyes though, like mint leaves, that brought me to be so distracted that I hit a solid chest.

Damn it. Second time. Second freakin' time. This time I wasn't as thrilled with who I had ran into. No, he reminded me of Jed. The guy looked down at me with a big grin that showed off far too large of teeth. "What do we have here?"

I heard his friends laugh, but my focus was on the predator in front of me. I felt my nails curl into my hoodie sleeves as I swallowed my fear. A wave of nausea rolled through me as panic set in. *What the hell was I doing here?* This was why I didn't belong around normal people. Hell, I didn't know the first thing outside of the basement I had grown up in. If it hadn't been for Pastor Malcolm's lessons and my mother's swearing, I would have been a freak. I mean I was a freak now, just slightly less of one.

"Sorry," I whispered through a raspy voice. Fuck. My voice wasn't used to being used. On top of that, after years of being forced to swallow acidic kitchen supplies, it may have been permanently damaged. The damage was the only part of me that didn't heal, no matter how much I bled.

"Don't worry babe, you can make it up to me," he leered with evident amusement.

"Or you can fuck off Lorn," a voice snarled behind me. I didn't recognize the voice, but my heart pitter-pattered at the dangerous sound. That familiar sense of safety crawled up my throat and caused me to open my mouth in surprise.

"This your girl or something?" Lorn, I assumed, snickered.

A warm bonfire scent invaded my nose as a large hand pressed into my lower back for support. I was surprised to find myself leaning back into it despite the pain. I looked up into a pair of deep indigo eyes that burned like embers in a fireplace. I noticed he wore a hoodie like me. Maybe we could be friends. I wouldn't mind a friend this tall or big. My brain and heart seemed to have frozen time to allow me to look at this handsome man. My new friend was so ridiculously good-looking. Something in the center of my chest was begging me to vie for his attention, but it didn't seem like I needed to. He was already paying attention.

"Yep," he answered smoothly. I wasn't positive what

'your girl' meant, but if it meant being friends, I was totally in. The more I looked at him, the more I liked him.

He had stark white skin that shone against black messy curls and dark brows. The ends of his curled hair were dipped in bright orange. It accented his feline face and full gentle lips. Those lips that looked nearly out of place on his masculine features. Overall, the effect was stunning.

This town had two good looking men, which was a record. Then again, my social experiences consisted of three people.

I stood corrected as another figure appeared on my other side. A small sound tumbled out as I looked at two matching people. *Twins.* My heart began to work overtime, the feeling of safety expanded and allowed for something more. It made my face flush as I resisted the urge to bounce on my toes with excitement. I felt hyper and manic. What the heck was going on with me? The back of my neck felt cool and my body hot with chills. Something inside of me fluttered around dangerously back and forth, back and forth.

"Alright Ledger," Lorn scoffed before leaving. I couldn't look away from the matching people though. My eyes trailed from their lean lethal bodies and categorized the small differences.

"He's such an asshole," the second one growled. I jumped just enough that his eyes snapped down to me and softened. The effect was beautiful.

Unlike his brother's indigo eyes, bright blue eyes like two crystals looked back at me. They were framed by thick dark lashes and matched the diamond piercing in his dark brow. The white polo he wore stretched across his shoulders, but didn't cover the shadow of extensive dark tattoos that trailed from shoulder to shoulder. I let my eyes wander on how they wrapped around his arms. I didn't understand the words within the tattoo, but found the swirled pattern to be comforting, almost reminiscent of something familiar. I noticed that they possibly extended over his shoulders and down his back. I found I wanted to trace each one of them until I met their end. It was like a shirt under a shirt.

"Anani." He offered a hand and flashed me a brilliant smile which reminded me of the lightning that use to bounce off the church grounds. I met his hand and was surrounded by the scent of electricity. It made me breathless.

"Maya," I mumbled. I was completely enamored.

"Ledger," the orange-tipped man offered. I noticed small differences between his brother and him. I couldn't tell if tattoos adorned his body because of the comfortable hoodie he wore. While Anani seemed to spark like something dangerous in the air, Ledger reminded me of strength and warmth. It was in his comfortable demeanor and oversized clothing. It encouraged me to trust him. Plus his orange-tipped hair reminded me of fire.

I bit my lip while looking between Anani and Ledger. How could they be twins? *One was clearly a lip-biting experience and the other a lazy Sunday afternoon. I had read about both in Cosmo!*

I really couldn't tell you what either of those really meant, but it just seemed like a good description and it matched the type of men shown pictured in the magazine. Cosmo magazine was one of the first things my mother had purchased on the road.

"Beautiful name for a heartbreaking woman," Anani winked, making me blush.

"So sorry about Lorn," Ledger explained softly after his brother finished, "he's a bit of an ass."

I smiled, "I gathered that, thanks for helping out."

"Your voice, are you sick?" Anani asked with a frown that didn't match his normal velvety voice.

I shook my head. I didn't offer more than that but smiled as the bell rang. I turned on my heel and glided away from the handsome men. I was thankful for them helping out, but had no idea what to say next. I felt like the normal thing to do was just to leave. That made sense, right?

"Maya," Ledger chuckled and spoke louder, "where are you going, Firefly?"

"Firefly?" I scrunched my nose up. Anani laughed as Ledger's easy smile grew bigger. There was a light pink to his cheekbones.

"Yeah, Little One, where are you going?" Anani tried instead. I frowned at that as well. I wasn't that little. I mean, I wasn't a giant like them, but 'Little One.' *Come on!*

"Class," I responded quietly with a head tilt. "Don't you have class as well?"

"With you, yes," Anani offered me a smile that made my chest bubble with excitement.

"How do you know my schedule?" I rose a brow.

Ledger chuckled but threw him a look. "Everyone knows what classes the new kid gets tossed into. We've been in school a week, so the teachers announced it."

I nodded. Maybe that was how that worked?

"Henry!" Ledger grinned knowingly. My head snapped from the relaxed yet playful twins to the person I assumed was Henry.

"Hey, guys," the more relaxed voice said from the closed door of the classroom, "and girl." His pale face flushed pink as the twins both chuckled. Henry was leaner than the twins, and shorter. Yet his chest and shoulder were built like the swimmer I had seen in the school's brochure. I wondered if he was a swimmer.

His hair was a soft blonde that waved over his light grey eyes. He had a pair of dark-framed glasses that seemed to glint slightly in the gloomy school lighting. I noticed the slight spatter of freckles that covered his pale nose. He was a total cutie.

"This is Maya," Anani winked at Henry. "Isn't she just the cutest?"

I heard a growl escape my lips that made all three of them freeze.

I flushed because I knew that sound often made an appearance when I was frustrated. It didn't help when they all broke into a fit of laughter. Loud laughter that echoed through the hall.

"She just growled." Anani could barely breathe with how hard he laughed.

"I'm in love," Ledger gasped while leaning into the lockers.

Henry's face was flushed from trying to stop his laughter as he shook his head almost embarrassed, "I'm sorry Maya, ignore us. We aren't used to being around women, especially those two."

I was still embarrassed so I nodded and walked toward the classroom. Henry followed after and I preened a little at the idea of them not being around women a lot. What made me special? Why did I get to be their friend? The three of them weren't nearly as intimidating as Marco. I could see myself spending a lot of time with my new friends.

If they wanted to be friends with the girl who growled, that was their choice.

The minute I entered the classroom late, my face returned to bright red once again. Henry placed a hand to my back as the four of us avoided the scowling look the teacher sent us. It was a gentle touch, but it still hurt my bruises. I didn't want him to ask questions though, so I didn't say anything.

"Mr. Asfour," the middle-aged man scowled, "if you and your brother would be so kind as to stop interrupting my class, I would be thankful."

Anani saluted him and followed in last. I sat down on a small desk chair as both twins sat to either side of me and Henry moved to sit behind me. His hand squeezed my shoulder in a reassuring way. I shot him a soft smile, trying to hide the pain his actions caused.

When I turned around, I noticed a woman with crimson hair staring at the four of us. Her eyebrows were bent in confusion. Not wanting enemies, I offered her a soft smile that she returned.

I wish I could have told you what class consisted of. I had been placed in average level classes, so the work seemed fairly simple. Instead, I was overwhelmed by the number of fresh scents around me. I recognized the electric and warm scents the twins put off, but the new scent of mint came from Henry. It was a fresh clean scent that reminded me of spring rain.

"Mr. O'Connor," the teacher, Mr. Fields, called on Henry. The class covered United States History from the time of World War I and on. Pastor Malcolm had been obsessed with World War II, so I felt fairly comfortable in the class.

When the bell finally rang, I moved from my seat and went toward the door. I noticed the three of them followed me as they talked casually about class. I turned and walked backward for a moment.

"If you're wondering," Ledger offered a lazy grin, "we are in all of your classes."

I frowned. I wasn't positive that was how school worked, but I did my best to keep my questions to myself. If they wanted to hang out with me that much, I wasn't going to complain.

Someone banged into me by accident and I hissed, but turned around to a hand steadying me. A pair of warm brown eyes stared down at me, his scent a soft forest one and his face handsome with soft black curly hair. He tilted his head in a way that reminded me of a dog.

"Sorry there." He didn't let go of me. Then he continued, "you must be new," the man said with an authentic smile, but I still felt nervous. It was clear he'd meant to run into me.

"I am. My name is Maya," I said softly, feeling uncomfortable.

A soft low sound came from behind me as the man offered a hand. "Well, Maya, I'm Seth. Sorry for bumping into you, you okay?"

I nodded as another growl ripped behind me. Seth looked up as his lip twitched. "I'll see you around?"

"Sure?" I whispered, feeling very confused, as he left. Now, I didn't know a ton about interactions, but that felt odd.

Instantly an arm was around my waist as I jumped and looked up. Anani shook his head muttering something before leading me towards our class. I was confused on why the boys looked upset.

They hadn't been lying. From US History through Chemistry, Calculus (which I found myself *bamboozled* by), to Policy class, they were in each one. Only Henry had disappeared at lunch time. The twins however, had led me to a back table where they dropped backpacks before grabbing their lunches from their bag. I sat there with a pleased expression on my face. The table offered a fantastic view of the garden that was in an open-air pavilion at the center of the school.

"Where's your lunch?" Ledger asked with a slight frown. My chest constricted because I really didn't like that upset look on his face.

I hummed and looked away, "Don't have one, we only eat dinner usually."

Both twins stilled in confusion.

"You can go buy one up there," Anani offered, throwing a thumb back at the long lunch line.

I flushed, licking my lips nervously. "I'll have to bring money tomorrow."

Why did this feel like a big deal?

Both twins frowned, Ledger pushing half of his sandwich toward me. It was made of a light bread and Peanut butter. I totally knew this type of food. See? *I was cool! I knew things!*

"So what's your plan after school, Peanut ?" Anani asked. I smiled at that nickname. Much better than 'Little One', although I was positive it meant the same thing to him. The 'Firefly' name was growing on me as well. I liked those little bugs, they use to fly in through the basement window and light up the room. My chest warmed at the positive memory buried within the others.

"Well, I'll probably walk around town for a bit before heading home," I offered casually. I was proud of that statement. It sounded like something a normal teenager would do. See? I'm just exploring the town. Not avoiding my trailer and abusive mother.

"You walk to school?" Anani sputtered. "It's freezing out."

Or not.

I tugged on my hoodie. "All warm and cozy, I promise."

Ledger frowned and pulled out a sleek black object before asking, "What's your number? We can pick you up each morning if you text us the address." Number? *Oh!* That was a phone, I'd read about those.

I blushed, a bit embarrassed I needed clarification. "Texting? You would need a phone to do that, right?"

Both eyes darkened slightly at my admission as I flushed a bright red. Before they could respond, a solid arm crashed over my shoulder and caused me to hiss in pain. I flinched and it didn't go unnoticed by either of the twins sitting across from me.

"Malloy," Anani snapped, "get your fucking arm off her."

The arm was instantly gone and a worried pair of of soft brown eyes appeared next to me. I frowned and scooted back just slightly. This guy didn't give me a bad feeling, but my back hurt like hell and I was worried my new friends would notice. Plus, he didn't make me feel like how Henry and the twins made me feel. This was more like the porridge that my mother used to give me on cold mornings.

"Now, what's a pretty girl like you doing, sitting with these jokers?" He chuckled with caution. I was concerned about his well-being. He was my size and taunting the large giants across the table. The pipsqueak would end up getting killed.

"Stop hitting on her," Ledger muttered.

I was naïve about the world. I knew that. However, in the past six days I had completely devoted myself to reading everything and anything. I had some general knowledge from homeschooling, but my cultural knowledge was absent. After reading a few magazines like Cosmo and a hefty stack of newspapers, I knew a little more than I used to.

For example, hitting on someone was what you did when you like them. I supposed I had never been hit on in my life before. Although the darkness, on those lonely nights in the basement, used to hold me. It used to comfort me.

God, I was a freak.

What would these boys think if they knew I had never been kissed? They wouldn't want to be my friend, I'll tell you that. Plus, I couldn't ignore the small excitement that fluttered through my stomach at the appearance of their smiles. I would probably never be normal enough for someone to like me, but at least I could have friends. The butterflies would have to go. Now, if only I could find something or someone to tell me how to get rid of them.

"Right, cuz that's what I was doing," Malloy rolled his eyes not looking bothered in the least, "where is Henry at?"

"Busy," Anani responded. His jaw was tense and those bright eyes trained at the place between Malloy and me. Ledger though was focused on my shoulders and face. Could he tell I had bruises? Crap. I hoped not.

The bell rang after a quiet lunch. The three of us walked toward gym as Ledger made a proposal, "Come hang out with us after school, Maya."

I nodded and agreed, "Sounds fun." Anani looked relieved and Ledger tossed me a small smile.

I walked into the female locker room and made my way to the coach's office. At least, that was what the schedule labeled her as. Coach Julie. The locker room was made out of this God awful yellow and green tile pattern and the showers leaked, causing my ears to ring slightly. I swallowed and knocked on the door as a woman with messy brown hair looked up at me. Her eyes were wide and her skin like tanned leather over a muscular athletic build. I was totally jealous of how strong she was.

"You must be Maya," the coach offered.

"Yes," I whispered, "I'm here to pick up my uniform."

"So you are," she sighed, checking something on her clipboard, "here you go."

I grabbed my uniform and went toward the changing area. Luckily, there were stalls. I stepped into one and opened my backpack. I peeled off my hoodie and hung it across the stall door. I stepped out of my skirt and pulled on the loose shorts and baggy shirt trying to avoid the gross water on the floor. I didn't want to ruin what nice clothes I had. Unfortunately, you could see a small amount of bruising on my bicep and neck. It wasn't terrible, but I knew it was enough that people would notice. I tugged back on my hoodie.

"There she is," Anani said with relieved expression. The three of them had waited outside my locker room. I tried to ignore some of the dirty looks the other girls offered me. I wasn't positive if it was something I'd done or if they didn't like my friends. Maybe both?

I smiled and then my mouth dipped. It was hot as heck in the gym. So hot the glass was fogging. Everyone stood in the center as I joined. I knew the teacher would notice my hoodie as soon as she caught my eye.

"Maya, I don't need anyone passing out. Hoodie off."
Oh crap.

I bit my lip but stepped back from the group to pull off the hoodie. No one except the boys paid me any mind as we received instructions for the day. I hoped my hair would cover the bruising on the back of my neck. I tried to pull off the hoodie carefully so my clothes wouldn't shift and reveal the bruising.

Ledger looked me over and his mouth tightened just enough to look distressed. Did he see them? My eyes shot to Henry and Anani. *Yeah.* They saw them.

Anani's eyes were blazing as Henry offered me a heartbreaking look. I ignored them and kept my eyes forward. *I needed a lie.* I knew they would ask the minute she was done talking. I didn't need anyone noticing the way my mother treated me. I only had 5 days left. 5 days until I never had to worry about it again.

"Alright today, I need you to jog 10 laps," the coach yelled. I waited until we began jogging in the back to open my mouth.

"What the hell are those?" Anani hissed before I could speak. His hand grasped my arm and pushed up my sleeve, I cringed at the sound that came out of his mouth. I wasn't scared of him, but the energy vibrating around him wasn't sweet and those eyes were enraged.

"Accident, I had a bad accident about," *my entire life,* "5 days ago. It's still healing."

Anani shook his head at my lie but kept quiet. Except for that rumble in his chest that had my heart racing and breathing quickening. Ledger spoke quietly, "What type of accident?"

The kind that gave birth to me.

"Fell down some stairs while moving," I muttered. I hated lying. I was terrible at it.

I felt a cool hand on my neck and knew it was Henry. His chest made a low rumble, but all hesitancy from earlier was wiped away as he peered at the skin. I could practically feel him thinking and the gaze he offered me was both clinical yet concerned.

"How bad is it?" Henry asked so softly I barely heard him.

"Bad enough," I responded, but then picked up from walking to jogging.

The rest of gym, they were quiet. I knew they didn't believe my lie. I didn't even believe me.

No one would want to be my friend if they knew how not normal I was. How awful my mom treated me. How I was possessed by the devil and that was why she had to hurt me. No one would even want to be around me.

I was glad these boys made me feel so comfortable because I wasn't sure how I would feel around other people. My experience with Seth and Lorn hadn't been good so far, and I hadn't talked to anyone else really. Well, Malloy I suppose, but he didn't leave me with a bad feeling, just sort of nothing. I was thankful for that in comparison to the intense pull and push of feeling strongly about the guys and the uncomfortable one I got around the other two. With my friends, I felt like an attention-starved kitten.

I'd always wanted a kitten. There used to be strays that would come to the window of the basement. One time, I'd even created a little corner for them to stay in during the winter. I'd been terrified my mother or Pastor Malcolm would realize they were down there, but they stayed quiet as their mother left to hunt each day and came back with rats and mice. She fed her children like a real mom was supposed to. I think that was when I realized how bad my situation was. When the six of them left one afternoon and never came back, I'd cried for three days straight, but it taught me that getting attached to things was something I couldn't afford.

Now that I was going to be free I wanted something I could be attached to. Something I could love. I really should get a kitten. That was the first order of business on my birthday.

After gym, securely changed into my clothes, I found the boys waiting for me. I had all my books with me because I wasn't positive where we would be going now that school was over. I knew I had homework, but I had never done any before, so I figured it was better to be safe than sorry.

"Come on," Anani offered in a slightly dimmer tone than before gym. I could see concern sparkling in his normally playful eyes. His warm hand met mine and squeezed it gently. I offered him a bright smile that had the light rekindling.

"Nice car," I offered. I knew nothing about cars. All I knew was that this one was shiny, big, and black. I struggled to get up into the seat so Ledger smiled and aided my effort. He walked around to the driver's side as both other boys hopped into the back.

As the car engine started up, my smile grew. This was exciting. This was a freakin' adventure. Maybe school wouldn't be that bad.

2
MAYA

"So what are we going to do?" I asked curiously after a few minutes of driving. I felt excited to be hanging out with real friends. At least, I assumed we were real friends. I didn't have any fake friends to compare them to.

"We wondered if you wanted to come do homework at our house," Henry offered, "if you don't want to, we can go to the library."

"Either way, we have to get it done or Marco will flip," Ledger sighed.

Marco? It couldn't be the same one, could it? I had to know.

"We can do your place." I beamed, my hands tangled together nervously. I wasn't nervous because of them, but at the prospect of doing something my mother didn't know about. What would she do if she found out?

The boys talked as they fidgeted with the heat and radio buttons. I took the time to examine the small coastal town I had found myself inhabiting. The sky was a cold gray color that reminded me of Henry's sparkling eyes. A storm seemed to be constantly a minute away. The air smelled of water and brine with seagull cries echoing from every stone surface we passed. Small but expensive cars littered the driveways of coastal homes and jacketed individuals hurried out of the wind into store fronts. Despite the gloomy atmosphere, or maybe because of it, I felt at home. I had felt a connection to this place the minute I had arrived here. I had to wonder if it was connected to my new friends at all because I couldn't imagine the place without them in it.

Something about all of this seemed unique. I didn't think most people had friendships like this.

"Holy crap," I muttered.

The house we pulled up to was as large as the massive church I had been locked up in. The slate gray walls and angular glass windows showcased a steely and cold front that complimented the natural environment. Thick lush greenery surrounded the building and reflected against the front windows. I immediately noticed that a familiar BMW sat in front of the house. After seeing Marco's car, I had asked my mother about the brand. Jed had sneered and said it was ass stupid foreign car. The fact that Jed hadn't liked it just made me like it more.

"It's Marco's home, but we all live here," Henry explained softly.

"I've met Marco," I admitted with almost certainty. "I recognize his car from the gas station the other day."

The entire car went silent as Ledger shifted into park. *I wish I knew how to drive.* That was on my checklist of things to do. I wondered if my new friends would teach me.

"That bastard," Anani finally chuckled, the sound making me perk up.

"Explains how he was acting," Henry muttered in a dry,

almost exhausted tone.

"Let's go give him shit," Ledger grinned, "come on, Firefly."

I frowned but followed after them. As I stepped up onto the slate gray stairs, I found myself peering into a massive stone door. It opened with an ease that I wasn't positive was possible.

"What are you guys doing home?" A voice rang out. It was deep and accented. A figure rounded the corner. "Be careful, Marco is all caught up on some- *Shit*."

"This is Firefly," Ledger offered quickly. "I have a feeling this explains *that*."

"Explains what?" I asked as my eyes fluttered around the room. It was too much to take in. Modern. So sleek and modern. Filled with floral arrangements and dark comfortable furniture. Very masculine, yet comfortable. I loved it immediately.

"Maya?" The voice asked. I focused on its sender and felt my eyes widen.

"How do you know my name?" I wondered out loud. There was no way this man knew my name. No one that beautiful should speak my ugly name. My mother had said it meant 'water' because it was the opposite of the Hell fire that burned inside of me. She was a peachy woman. Really.

"Marco mentioned you, but he left out that you're our-"

"Friend," Anani interrupted. "She's our friend. Maya, aka Peanut , and is very unaware of our family dynamic, Sai."

"What family dynamic?" I asked curiously.

Sai stunned me. He had beautiful obsidian hair that hung to his shoulder in soft curls and sparkling black eyes. There was an element to his face that spoke to fire and passion. Maybe it was his structured jaw or stunning white smile. His entire demeanor was smoky and hot. It was like someone had lit a flame and it had turned into this muscular tall man. Even his skin was burnt into a beautiful deep tan.

"Just that we all live together," he muttered with darkening eyes and stepping forward. The scent of cinnamon surrounded me like warm flames. I swayed toward him as those large hands grasped my shoulders gently. I hissed just slightly under the pain, but it almost didn't matter.

"Why do you have bruises?" He demanded with a spark of temper I hadn't expected. I snapped out of my trance and stepped back. I swallowed and spoke my lie.

Sai frowned and met Henry's eyes. Both of them exchanged a look.

"Marco," Anani finally called out. Even his name sent shivers through me.

From somewhere upstairs, a door slammed open. I cringed. The house had an open square ground floor that had cool slate flooring and massive ceilings. Everything was cold except the furniture that was styled in dark comfortable textiles. I couldn't see more than the corner of the kitchen from where I stood. Although, a massive staircase led to the top floor and through the open steps I could see a massive glass panel view of the forest. I could hear footsteps echoing down onto the landing.

I snapped my head up and found a familiar pair of mint green eyes.

In a movement so quick I knew it wasn't normal, my body was pressed into the scent of vanilla and pine. *I sighed into it.* I was even okay with the pain from his massive hands biting into my back. The room was still except for the deep rumble that echoed through Marco's chest and up my spine. His nose trailed in my hair as my knees buckled just slightly. A flame that I didn't know existed roared to life inside my small heart. I could barely breathe. Tears collected in my eyes slightly as I gripped his shirt, feeling a burst of pure joy at seeing him again.

"Holy shit Marco," Sai mumbled, "you could have told us."

Marco didn't respond, but instead tugged me tighter against his body. My hands curled into his crisp soft buttoned shirt even further. He was so much larger than I remembered. Was this normal? My reaction didn't feel normal, but at the same time, it was natural.

"Be careful Marco, she has bruises and you're holding her pretty tight." Henry's words brought a sound from Marco that sounded like a growl. I knew that sound, I growled sometimes. I pulled back to see if he was frustrated.

Those green eyes looked down at me and all the composure that had been there yesterday disappeared. His massive hand smoothed the back of my neck in gentle strokes as my eyebrows shot up. What in the heck was going on? My pulse was moving like butterfly wings and an infusion of warmth saturated through me.

"Are you okay?" He asked, his brow dipped in concern. There was a tightness in his jaw I didn't like. I brought my hand up to smooth his clean-shaven jaw.

A rumble started up in Marco's chest that had my eyebrows raising. Instead of lying, I continued to smooth my hand on his neck. I could feel myself melting into him as certain parts of him grew harder against me.

Now *that* I had read about in Cosmo. Oh. Also, after reading about Adam and Eve, mother had graced me with the birds and bees conversation. I didn't want to tell Marco I noticed, but I was pretty damn sure it meant he liked me. It was the physical equivalent of hitting on me. I wish I could warn him that I wasn't even worthy of friendship.

"Are you purring?" Anani chuckled so hard he gasped, holding his stomach.

"Shut it," Ledger smacked his head, "you were practically shifting at gym."

Henry smiled, "Accurate."

"How about I make you some tea?" Sai asked me from next to Marco. I looked away from the massive man and peered at Sai. Marco made a frustrated noise as if he was upset I looked away from him.

"What's tea?"

The room silenced, Sai frowned, and asked "You don't know what tea is?"

"She doesn't have a cell phone either," Anani commented. I shot him a scowl and wiggled away from Marco. He grumbled and hooked an arm around my waist gently. I settled facing the group.

"Can we not talk about what I don't have?" I frowned at Anani.

"Yeah Anani, stop being an ass," Ledger chuckled. He winked at me as Sai jerked his head toward the kitchen. I followed and stepped down into the main room that attached to the kitchen. It didn't escape my notice that Marco was plastered to my back still. Sai sighed and shook his head at Marco's rumbling chest. I didn't mind at all, in fact, I was more comfortable than I'd ever been in my entire life. It sounded naive, even to me, but with Marco right there in addition to my new friends in the same room... I felt the safest I'd ever felt in my entire life. Silly, right?

"Get her a cell phone," Marco spoke quietly to Henry. The man in question looked at me, his ears turning slightly pink, and sped from the room. It was still faster than normal. *Was I the only one noticing this?*

"Wait!" Ledger called out before looking back at me. "Any color preference?"

Henry peaked his head back over the stairs and explained, "They come in red, pink, black, and blue."

I smiled, "Pink, please." I blushed a little because Henry nodded quickly with a cute grin before rushing away. He made the butterflies jump in my stomach as well. There was an underlying vibration of energy coming off him that I didn't completely understand. I felt like he was hiding half of himself and I was very interested in knowing what that other half was.

"What flavor do you want?" Sai asked as Marco picked me up and placed me on top a large granite slab.

I didn't answer right away because the granite kitchen made me flustered. I shouldn't be in a kitchen like this and I shouldn't be on the counter. Kitchens like this only existed in the paper. The church kitchen had been small, and the only way I knew that was because a picture of it hung in the basement. At one time, it had been filled with a parish celebrating someone's baptism. I'd never been baptized because the minute that water had touched my skin, my mother had claimed I'd lit on fire.

It sounded very extreme, right? Not sure I believed her.

Sai presented me with three different shiny packs. One was orange, one purple, and the last green. I hesitantly pointed at the purple.

"Can we get a look at those bruises, Peanut ?" Anani asked with a small smile, but his eyes were dark as night.

I looked to Ledger, who offered a soft smile and began pulling food out of the fridge. My stomach rumbled on cue as Marco frowned. His ridiculously pretty face turned very serious.

"I'm making her food, relax Marco," Ledger sighed at

the man, "Firefly here shared our lunch, and tomorrow, I'm going to just pack her one. Apparently, they only eat dinner at her house."

"Where are you living?" Marco demanded his voice rough from the strain of his reactions. He had stepped between my legs and didn't look away from my face. Not even for a heartbeat. "I tried searching for you, but the rain had washed away the scent of the car. I'm sorry I didn't find you sooner."

I swallowed, blushing at his sweet comment. *This man had been looking for me?* I nibbled my lip and spoke, "Um, I don't know what the trailer park is called, Jed…"

A cup crashed onto the counter as Sai turned and exclaimed, "You live in a fucking trailer?"

I cringed. Lord help me if he ever finds out I lived in a basement. Apparently, that wasn't the norm outside of my previous life.

"It's not bad," I muttered feeling embarrassed.

"Sai, stop it," Marco snapped at him, "now Maya, who is Jed?"

I looked up at him and sighed, "My mom's boyfriend, we just moved here. You… eh, you met him at the gas station."

"Where's your dad?" Sai wondered out loud, his voice almost pleading to tell him some good news. So I did.

I hid my grin and said, "Dead."

"Maya, I'm so sorry." He froze, looking horrified.

"Please, please, don't be." I admitted with a voice that sounded cold even to me. All of them seemed to freeze at my words and they exchanged looks. *See?* I was already messing up this being normal thing.

"What time do you need to be home tonight?" Anani asked. *Did they want me to leave already?*

"Um," I frowned. "Honestly, I don't know how any of this works. This is my first time doing any of this."

"Any of what?" Ledger wondered.

"This," I motioned, "I had never left my... house until five days ago."

Silence spread across the room before Sai swore. He set down a cup of tea, a deep red shade, before storming off. I frowned, *was he mad at me?* I hoped not. I didn't mean to upset him.

"Not mad at you," Marco muttered while pressing a soft kiss to my shoulder, "just worried."

Could he read minds?

"I need to get a good look at her bruises," Ledger finally demanded, before pressing a sandwich into my hand. He wandered off before I heard him sorting through a closet down the hall.

Anani moved next to Marco, "Peanut, are you okay with that?"

I bit my lip but nodded as Marco stepped back. I tugged on the sleeve of my hoodie and pulled it over my head with gentle movements. I knew they were visible along my arms and open neckline because of the growl that came from Ledger. How could I tell them apart after only a few hours?

His eyes were burning as he grasped my hand gently. Marco had a vice grip on the counter as he muttered a curse, "How the hell did this happen?"

I looked down at the bruises covering my arms as Ledger moved around the counter, sliding onto the surface to sit behind me. I hissed as his warm hands traced the pattern through my thin white polo.

"I fell-"

"No, you didn't," Ledger hissed unexpectedly. "Come look at this Marco."

Marco already looked like he was about to explode. His eyes were trained on my bruised arm as his body trembled with anger. I curled into Ledger with repressed anxiety. I didn't think he would hurt me, but his energy was intense.

"Marco, calm down," Henry demanded from the door. He walked forward, gray eyes turning into melted silver, as he set down a pink phone on the counter. *Oh, I loved that color.*

"Eat," Ledger encouraged me quietly while the other two had a near stare off. I could practically see the conversation the two of them were having.

Marco sighed shaking his head, before he lifted and turned me. I was sitting sideways on the counter as Marco gently peeled my polo up. I cringed at his growl before Ledger softly massaged my hands in a comforting gesture. I took a bite of the sandwich. When I felt Henry's warm yet rough fingers pressing against the skin gently, I relaxed a bit. Maybe it came from my experience growing up, but it was far more reassuring knowing where someone's hands were, even if they were on me. When you didn't know where they were, you could be surprised. My mother liked to do that, hitting me out of nowhere.

"Who?" Henry pleaded. His voice was soft and silky as he rounded to stand in front of me.

"Why do you say who?" I muttered.

Henry's eyes darkened, "I have seen enough subcutaneous bruises to know which ones are caused by accidents and which are caused by human infliction. So who, Maya?"

Was it just me or was this guy really smart? He sounded like the anatomy book I'd read this past summer.

I shook my head and bit my sandwich. "Please leave it alone."

I could feel tears welling behind my eyelids as my lashes

fluttered. Marco pulled the shirt back down and lifted me into his arms. Do all friends carry one another? There was no way I was carrying these guys. I mean, I really would if I could, but they were huge. I rubbed my nose against his warm neck as he rumbled in that deep purr again.

Once I was situated in Marco's arms in what he deemed the family room, he sat down and Ledger offered me a blanket and my tea. I continued to nibble on my sandwich as Henry sat down. I knew I was taking advantage of their friendship, but this was the most comfortable I'd ever been. I briefly noticed the three other men talking in quiet whispers from the kitchen. They sounded worked up, but I hoped they would figure out what was bothering them.

"Okay, so put your finger here," Henry instructed. I could tell he was frustrated, but thankfully he had dropped the conversation from before. For now at least. The screen lit up and filled in a huge thumbprint with my own. I smiled at the idea.

"Now it will only open to you," he muttered and met my eyes.

I frowned, thinking about my lack of knowledge, "Can you put multiple thumbprints?"

Henry nodded and I smiled, "Please put everyone's thumbprint, I don't want to have to always open it for you guys if you need something."

Henry's eyes softened as Marco spoke in a voice that still seemed tense, "I have no idea what's going on at home Maya, but it would be best to hide this. I don't want anyone taking it away." I didn't know what to say, but I could tell Henry was preloading some data that probably had to do with what I asked for. I wanted my friends to be able to do what they needed.

I nodded, "Okay. So what is this for?" I was talking about the phone of course.

Henry frowned as Marco muttered something in a different language and answered, "It's a way to contact us." *Neat.*

He showed me how to text and call. I scrolled through six names, Atlas was the only one I didn't recognize. I assumed there was a good reason for including him. I sent out a text with smiley faces to all their phones. I jumped at the sound of bings through the room. Marco chuckled quietly. I really liked the sound coming out from his mouth.

"You didn't have to buy this," I muttered, "it's way too much." It was pink though. So pretty. I loved the color pink. It was the color of the roses that bloomed near the church's base and the color of the fading sunset. I loved those shades. Pinks, purples, oranges. Especially red. I would keep the phone for now, but only because I knew it was important to my friends. I wasn't positive why though.

"Consider it giving us peace of fucking mind," Sai snarled before coming to sit in front of Marco and me. He leaned his head back to look at me. I lifted a hand to comb through his hair and while his eyes flared in surprise, he relaxed into the motion.

"You guys are being really sweet," I untangled myself from Marco, but the man didn't let go of me, he kept a hand in mine, "do friends normally act like this?"

All five of them shifted uncomfortably as Anani spoke after a moment, "Peanut, have you ever had any friends like us?"

I shook my head. I had a response to this. "Nope. I have only known Pastor Malcolm, mother, and Jed."

"You mean those have been your only friends?" Henry clarified.

I frowned and explained, "No, like those are the only three people I have ever met. Well, I suppose after today that has expanded slightly..."

Sai cracked the table he had his hand on in front of us, the wood splintering before he stormed off. Ledger sighed and jogged after him as Anani grunted before following. Henry bit his lip and moved his gaze to the window portrait that faced the front of the house.

"Where did you move from?"

"Louisiana," I stated proudly.

"Who is Pastor Malcolm? Where did you live there?" Marco demanded with enough force to pop me out of my sense of security.

I knew he wouldn't want the answer to these questions. I sighed, "Pastor Malcolm was my father, and he's dead now." I just ignored the other question.

The room was quiet. I stood up, finally escaping his comforting grip, and walked toward the large glass window that featured the impressive front driveway and forest landscape. The rain had begun in earnest and caused a fine fog to filter through the area. It was beautiful.

I liked these boys. Men? Men. But they were asking a lot of questions and I didn't think friends did this only a day after meeting. Plus, biology told me Marco might like me. That was a problem. They were really nice and didn't deserve to be deceived. At the same time, I can't exactly tell them how worthless I was. If my mother were here, she would have done a much better job.

I knew there was only one solution and it broke my heart.

I would have to give up my new friends. I mean, I didn't want them to get hurt by accident. My mother was really violent and I didn't want them to get caught in the cross hairs. I turned with determination.

"We can't be friends," I announced, "I don't want you to get hurt."

Henry paled and looked to Marco.

The man blinked three times before shaking his head in shock. "I don't know if I should be fucking pissed your life is that dangerous or amused that you think we could get hurt."

I frowned, feeling frustrated. "Marco, I know all of you are massive giants, but there are a lot of big people out there and while I will always cherish my first friendships..."

Marco chuckled and remarked, "Amused it is then. Also, giants?"

I shrugged and replied, "I'm pulling from the Bible and fairytales here. So either giants or dragons, you pick."

Marco offered a wicked smile as Henry shook his head as he answered, "Dragons."

Henry smiled with strain before approaching me. "Listen, Maya, you really don't need to worry about us. I promise you, we won't get hurt."

I frowned. "But-"

"Trust me?" Henry pleaded. His fingers slipped into mine as I looked down at our hands. I nodded because when it was just Henry and I, my body felt a bit like honey. Sweet and slow.

I didn't trust him. Well, *I did*. But he clearly didn't know what was good for himself.

"Fine," I sighed. "I'll just have to protect you all."

Marco let out a booming chuckle while Henry smiled softly. "How about you protect us and we will protect you as well? It's what friends do."

I pursed my lips, contemplating and said, "Okay deal.

Plus I don't know how to handle people like that Lorn guy." Marco snarled from the couch at my expression.

Henry frowned, "What happened with Lorn?"

"She accidentally bumped into him and he... was being difficult," Ledger muttered while followed by Sai and Anani.

Sai scooped me up into a soft hug and muttered, "Sorry."

I patted his head before pulling back, "Thank you." No idea what he was apologizing for, but that was what you did when someone said 'sorry.'

"Did he just apologize?" Anani hooted. "That's amazing."

"Shut it," Sai growled.

Marco stood with a grunt, "Sai come with me, and you four should start some homework." *That wasn't a half-bad idea.*

I frowned at his possible departure, but he walked over and pressed a kiss to my forehead. I preened under his affection like the starved woman I was. Sai hugged me lightly, careful to not press any bruises before they went to the foyer.

"Where did they go?" I asked Henry with unabashed curiosity.

He looked away, "Um, an errand I think." *Now why did that ring partially false?*

I nodded and gripped his hand again. He blushed but I didn't care. We both walked toward the kitchen. I picked up the mug of tea and took a long sip. I hummed my approval at the taste, reminding me of berries that grew outside the church basement window. I voiced that description.

"Why were you in a church basement?" Ledger asked quietly after a moment.

I froze and took another drink, "It was near our house." Sorta. Okay, it was my house.

"I thought you had never really left your house?" Anani narrowed his eyes.

"We lived in the church," I muttered.

Henry squeezed my hand, "So why were you in the basement?"

"Can we not talk about this?" I forced out, feeling a bubble of panic, "Please? I'm really tired."

I hopped onto the kitchen stool and pulled out my books, ignoring the glances they shared. The books were second hand, but smooth to the touch. I opened a small black notebook that was labeled 'planner'. It had come in the package with my uniform and books. I wondered how Jed afforded to send me to school.

"Oh what are those?" I pointed to Anani's planner. I noticed that he was dressed differently now. A black tank covered his muscular top and a pair of jeans fitted to him covered the bottom. He was the only one who had changed out of the four of us.

"Stickers," he grinned, "want some?"

"Absolutely," I responded.

Anani opened a few drawers and pulled out several packs. I sorted through several dark packs before finding one with flowers. I opened them with a delicate touch, then placed them in an even pattern that brightened up the surface. It was stunning.

"You're sort of a girly girl," Ledger teased.

I smiled and asked, "What's that?"

Henry hummed, "It's like a girl that loves pink and wears dresses, although I've only seen you in black. Plus, the concept of being a 'girly girl' is a grossly antiquated concept."

"I'm not retracting my statement," Ledger grinned.

"I only own some stuff we picked up at the store called Goodwill on the way out here," I reasoned in reference to his black clothing comment. Anani made a sound that had me looking up.

"What about your clothes before?" Ledger tilted his head that frown line between his brows deepening.

I opened and closed my mouth, "Well, I only had two dresses at my old home." There, that seemed normal enough.

Henry whispered, "And now?"

"My uniform, one pair of PJs, two pairs of sweatpants, a hoodie, and the two dresses," I listed my fast growing collection of clothes.

Henry pressed his lips together and immediately asked, "Do you want more?"

I frowned, "I don't think mother would like that."

"What if you kept them here?" Ledger reasoned.

"Maybe," I sighed distracted by my stickers, "but then I would need to purchase them somehow."

"Give me your wallet, we can put one of the cards-" Anani demanded. I raised my brows.

"Wallet?"

"Where do you keep your ID, honey?" Henry mumbled quietly.

"I don't have one of those," I frowned again. *I really hated feeling like I had no idea what the heck was going on.*

"Fuck," Anani muttered with a groan, "sort this out please?" Henry nodded and opened his laptop.

"I don't need one, I can't drive," I explained.

"How have you lived this long without any of this? I mean, you would have had to be locked up your entire life." Anani's words brought a flush to my cheeks.

"Something like that," I mumbled. Ledger hit him in the side while Henry offered me an alarmed look.

"What type of wallet do you want?" Anani asked while pulling up a site on my phone. He offered me an apologetic smile at his outburst. Henry had very much caught what I'd mumbled and I mentally cursed for revealing so much. It was very difficult being around these men and keeping secrets. There was this oddly instinctual part of me that begged me to trust them and to answer their questions honestly. Then there was the rational part of me that knew it could put them in harm's way, or make them not want to be my friend.

"What is this?"

"Amazon," he explained, "you can buy anything you want on it. You just have to know what you are searching for."

"I don't have money."

All three guys exchanged a look, Henry spoke, "don't worry about that, just use the card and address listed."

"I don't want to use your money," I shook my head.

"Not ours," Ledger smiled.

"Whose is it?"

"Marco's account, he won't mind."

I frowned because this didn't seem right, "And you say I need this stuff?"

Anani nodded and confirmed, "You need a wallet, you already have a phone and Henry will work on the ID for you."

I flushed, "Um okay. So what type of wallets are there?"

For the next hour, the four of us looked through this Amazon store. I picked out a beautiful pink wallet that had daisies embroidered on the front of it. I had thought it had been enough, but the boys added a few more things into the cart I'd pointed out. I smiled at the phone case and fuzzy slippers. Both were pink and the phone case featured a bow. I instantly loved it. I also found I loved glitter. Who the heck could live without glitter in their life? Now that I'd found it, I wanted to toss glitter onto and into everything. Maybe I'd put it on all my clothes.

"This weekend we will pick you up some new clothes," Anani assured me.

I frowned, "I need a job then."

Anani sighed, "No mate of ours is going to work."

"Mate?" I voiced.

"Like a friend," Henry muttered. Anani grunted as Ledger hit him upside the head.

"Oh, a character from one of my books called his friend that," I explained.

"What books have you read?" Henry mused.

"Oh, a bunch of stuff. Let's see, since we left I have read some newspapers and magazines. Pastor Malcolm used to give me text books to read. He called it my homeschool time."

Henry sputtered, causing me to look up. "That was your homeschooling?"

I raised a brow. "Well, I didn't have much to do besides reading and learning. Although, that calculus class goes way beyond the math I studied."

"You taught yourself?" Ledger asked.

I chuckled, "How else would I learn?" Then the sad reality hit me that these boys had worked with teachers probably most of their lives. A slice of misplaced envy tousled through me.

I looked outside to hear thunder sound through the forested area. "Hey, I should really get home. I didn't realize how bad it was out there."

"Okay," Ledger voiced after they exchanged a look, "do you want dinner before you leave?"

I shook my head, "I'll be okay." *I couldn't have them thinking I didn't eat dinner either.*

Ledger frowned, his dark brown hair brushing across his forehead, as Anani rounded the counter. He grabbed a set of keys as the four of us strolled through the house toward a small door. My backpack was neatly organized and on my shoulders. I occasionally winced at the feeling, but attempted to ignore it.

"Here, let me," Henry offered with soft stormy eyes. I nodded as he slipped the bag onto his own shoulders and led me to a large black SUV.

"Do you have your phone?" Ledger asked with a tightness around his mouth.

I held up my phone as Henry took it, pressing a small button that adjusted the ringtone to silent. Additionally, he dimmed the lighting. I offered him a sweet smile.

The roads were flooded with rain water and a dark sky rolled above us in anger. It reminded me briefly of the stormy nights the church's power would go out. Those were the worst. No lights. No heating. Not that the basement had much to begin with, but something was always better than nothing.

Anani turned around in a sharp movement and pleaded, "Don't go home."

I rose a brow. "What? Why?" *I totally didn't want to.*

Those diamond eyes glittered with anger and I instinctively flinched back. It was aimed at me, but didn't seem to be about something I had done. Anani's eyes then shone with guilt seeing my reaction and softly explained, "I just would feel better if you weren't at a damn trailer park."

I blushed in embarrassment and stammered, "I mean, I know it's not like your house..."

Ledger scoffed and hit his twin on the head. The two of them seemed to bop each other on the head a lot. Or was that just me? "Ignore him, Maya. This isn't about where you live. He's just worried about you and is shit at showing it."

I frowned before twisting my hands in my lap and murmuring, "Really, I'm fine."

Somehow the boys found their way to my trailer park. I bit my lip as I directed them down the lane toward a stone-colored trailer, the laminate sides drenched from the rain and the windows screaming with darkness. I knew Jed wasn't home, the truck was gone, but that didn't mean my mother wasn't inside.

"We will pick you up tomorrow," Ledger spoke gently but very confidently. I nodded because I didn't want my new friends to be upset. I just hoped mother or Jed wouldn't notice.

I slid from the truck and paused. "Thanks for everything." It was muttered and my cheeks were bright pink, all three of them traded small smiles with me. I trudged up the wooden steps toward the rickety front door. I offered them a small wave.

The trailer smelled of cigarettes and alcohol. I wasn't particularly used to the smell, the church hadn't smelt like that, but I was growing used to it. Jed smelled like that. I hated it.

"Where the fuck have you been?" A raspy feminine voice asked me. I squinted in the darkness of the trailer. I dropped my bag onto the floor.

Everything was the same from this morning. I could see the shattered plate I had dropped this morning, after the first hit, laying in the dusty kitchen. I categorized the yellow cabinets, shag carpeting, and dated furniture. I looked for Jed and any other threats, before looking at my mother.

I flinched at how tall she was compared to me. Her body was much larger than my own and covered in a sweaty nightgown. I examined her white-blonde hair that always made me question my darker hair, instead of making eye contact.

"Where Maya?!" She screamed. My back hit into the trailer wall as thunder erupted from outside. I could feel something jabbing into my back. I groaned at the sensation of blood dripping down my school skirt. At least I would be healed by morning. Thank God for the nail sticking out.

I swallowed and rasped out, "Study group."

"Whoring yourself out more likely. I saw the men who dropped you off."

I shook my head, "No, just study partners, mom. They didn't want me to walk back in the rain."

She growled, a manic look in those dark eyes as her hand snaked forward to grab me by my hair. "Liar!" I hated that look in her eye, it was the one that made her think she was doing the right thing by hitting me, by purging the devil from me. Jed just seemed to take advantage by joining in on the action.

I groaned as her hand tightened on my hair. She dragged me toward the kitchen sink and yanked open a cabinet. The cabinet I had filled after unpacking. She placed a bottle of hand soap onto the counter.

"Clean your mouth out, now," she snarled. "Liars are impure. Sinner."

I began to whimper as she poured the soap into my mouth, filling it with water and making me choke on the bubbles. I couldn't control my gut reaction to expel it. I felt the bile rise as my stomach forced out my sandwich from lunch onto my mother. I swore internally. Shit. Shit. Shit.

"You disgusting bitch," she raged. "That's God removing your sin!"

I let out a strangled sob as she dragged me to the ground, in the throw-up, and kicked me in the ribs. I gasped as something snapped. I could barely breathe as the intense pain radiated through me. She wasn't done though. Never done. Never enough.

My mind blanked with the singular hit to my back. I knew this punishment. Pastor Malcolm had done it often. I swallowed back the pain as my eyes found my backpack, only a bit away. My phone was in the side pouch and turned inward. I stared at it, attempting to draw strength from the thoughts of my new friends.

I had no idea how long she hit me.

When the door opened, I realized my mother had stopped. She talked with Jed, a happy lilt to her voice as my consciousness began to fade. I couldn't look at Jed and he made no mention of me. Instead, they began getting ready for dinner.

As if I wasn't lying on the floor in my own puke and blood.

I groaned as the door closed, waking me from my half-unconscious state. I watched the truck's headlights fade as I stumbled to my feet. I let out a small string of curses before looking to the floor. I shook my head with disgust before pulling off my shredded hoodie. I had no idea what I would wear to cover the bruises in the future.

I ripped the hoodie up further and began to clean up the mess at a painfully slow pace. My back was shredded and polo ruined. Once the hideous flooring was cleared of blood and vomit I stumbled toward the bathroom. I cringed while pulling off my skirt and was thankful that it only needed a wash. Only my upper body had gotten super bloody. Lucky me.

The shower stall was small. I turned on the warm water and rinsed my skirt in the sink before hanging it on a small towel rack. I looked at my pale form in the mirror before taking off my bra and underwear. I could see how bad the injuries were, but couldn't find a place inside of me to care. Why care when nothing would change? I could numb out the pain. It had happened so many times before and my skin was healing. I didn't think I had the devil inside me, but my mother did and until she didn't, this would keep happening. Only 4 days left.

The only thing keeping me going right now were thoughts of my new friends.

I didn't want to worry them. *Not that I wanted to assume they would worry, of course.* Still, I knew they were texting me, I could hear it while I laid on the floor. I wasn't positive how I had heard a silent notification, but I had.

The water was painful. I attempted to clean myself, especially my hair, of the puke and blood. Once I was finished, I walked naked toward my room and brought my skirt along. I opened a small window to let it air dry.

I couldn't call my room a bedroom now that I had seen the boy's house. It was a small space. I had a singular window and my mattress laid in the corner with a threadbare thrift store sheet on it. I pulled on a loose PJ shirt. I didn't want to get blood on any of my nice items. My steps took me back toward my backpack as I dragged it toward my bedroom. I locked the door and turned on the small light from the floor next to my bed. I ignored the spiders in the corner of the room.

Ledger: Text me when you are settled for the night,

Firefly.

Anani: Peanut? Please answer.

Henry: Are you alright Maya?

Sai: Maya, answer.

Marco: If I don't get a response in five minutes, I'm coming by.

I jumped to text them back. I didn't want my friends to see me like this.

Maya: I'm okay.

I breathed before my phone began to light up with a call. I picked up.

"Hello?" I asked into the small smooth contraption.

"Thank God," Marco muttered. "Why weren't you responding?"

I didn't want to lie, so I whispered, "I was with my mom."

I heard grumbling the background but Marco sighed. "I understand. All of us were just concerned about you."

I flushed at their thoughtfulness. "That's sweet of you all."

Marco grunted, "You will let the twins pick you up tomorrow."

I knew it wasn't a question, but still answered, "Yes, but can you tell them to meet me near the front of the trailer park? My mother was upset I hung out with boys."

Sai muttered something in the background before Anani told him to shut it. Marco grunted again, "Yeah, that's fine. How mad was she?"

I swallowed my lie, and replied, "She ended up going out with Jed, so apparently not terribly."

"You're home alone?" He asked quietly.

"Um," I bit my lip, "for a bit. I was about to head to

bed."

Marco sighed, "Okay. Atlas is in the area, he may stop by."

"I don't think that's a great idea, what if they come home?" I reasoned with panic.

"He is particularly quiet," Marco offered softly.

I mumbled back, "Okay, I may be sleeping though."

"That's okay," he stated. "Do you need anything?"

I didn't like the idea of someone I didn't know showing up while I slept, but Marco trusted him. Plus, I didn't believe men that huge could be sneaky, unless he was smaller. It was unlikely though. I looked at my tiny window and shook my head.

I bit my lip, considering. Then squeaked out, "Do you by chance have another polo for school?"

Silence followed.

"Why do you need a new polo?" Marco barely got out.

I thought fast, "Dinner." I *had been* in the kitchen.

Marco sighed in relief but hesitantly responded, "I will have Atlas drop one by."

I nodded. "Thank you. Tell everyone I say goodnight." I hated lying. I hated it. I forced myself to be good at it. They would have been so upset if they found out about the darkness that talked to me. The one in the center of my chest that told me to exact revenge. I suppose that was better than the one that told me to give up.

Marco repeated my message before whispering goodnight to me as well. I hung up the small pink device before placing it under my pillow. I closed my eyes in relief while positioning myself on my stomach. I hoped Atlas would just leave the polo at my window or something. I wasn't much in the mood for meeting anyone today.

It had been a very long day.

3
ATLAS

I moved silently through the trailer park, my motorcycle boots making barely a sound. I had parked a block away so to not attract attention. Inside my thick dark jacket was Maya's replacement polo. I wasn't positive I bought her story that Marco had told me, so I was glad to be taking a look.

As an enforcer to Marco's alpha, I was naturally suspicious. Of what? Everything. I sure as hell didn't know what to think about this girl that Marco was claiming as our mate. I knew the alpha felt the pull stronger at first, but I couldn't deny my concern at the slight figure being pulled into the dark truck at the gas station.

I hadn't seen her yet. I could tell she was beautiful from the way the other men talked about her, but nothing prepared me for seeing her in person. I rounded the trailer, checking the driveway, before going toward a small open window.

I knew I would be able to fit through it, but my eyes caught on the small school skirt hanging on the ledge. I moved closer and sniffed it. It smelled feminine, but also had the faint scent of blood. I examined the edge and noticed slight staining. My jaw tightened as I glided over the window with graceful ease.

Fuck.

Why had she left *this* window open? I could barely stand upright. The moon shone into the small closet and onto a mattress. Twin size. I felt my eyes widen in shock as I took in a delicate sleeping form. This was her fucking bedroom?

I felt an array of emotions coursed through me. Anger. Fury. Concern. Possession. Lust. My knees broke as I knelt down to the small Angelic form sleeping on a thin barely-there mattress. They hadn't been joking, she was beautiful. Yet, my appreciation was clouded by rage filtering over my eyes. Why the fuck was she sleeping here?

I wanted to take her to my room and let her sleep in my bed. Any of our beds actually. Just not here. Her thick dark hair laid in a seaweed mess on top of her stretched out arms. A tiny splattering of freckles covered her little nose and those long lashes swept across her high cheekbones. She was the most delicate, beautiful woman I had ever met. Hell. I hadn't even met her and every protective bone in my body was urging me to get her the fuck out of here.

I frowned though. I could feel my dragon's natural reaction to her, wanting to blanket her in protective and possessive actions, but he was blocking something. I wanted to ask the other men how people had been reacting to her. My senses told me that we were in a world of trouble. I had never smelled her unique mixture of soft scents, but I could tell she was a shifter, just no idea what type.

Maya muttered in her sleep before slipping from under her thin blanket. I groaned at her lack of clothing. Despite her loose t-shirt, it was clear she had shed off a pair of PJ pants. It made her little curves visible because she was in only a pair of panties. I tried to not look at her long legs and a tiny waist. How was it possible for someone so cute and small to be perfectly curved?

I really needed to not be staring at her. Then something caught my eye.

"What the fuck?" I growled. Her white shirt stuck to her back as a pale pink color began to seep through. Maya whimpered but continued to sleep. I moved slowly to peel her shirt off her back. I sucked in a breath.

Her entire back was covered in open wounds that looked like they originated from a belt. They were half healed, but bleeding still. I watched in amazement as her skin stitched itself up with a quickness that was obviously supernatural. I could feel a cold sweat take over her body as those small hands began to tremble. A pained sound came from her throat as my resolve melted.

In a movement that was quick but far from practiced, I pulled her onto my lap with a blanket in tow. I didn't touch her, except for a hand on her shoulder. Maya, still asleep, curled into my chest as a sigh of contentment came forth. I smiled at how perfectly she fit into my arms.

I could almost forget the terrible wounds on her back.

Almost.

4

MAYA

When I woke in the morning, I first noticed the warmth that radiated underneath my cheek. I sighed happily before snuggling into my bed's comfortable heat. My bed was totally more comfortable in the morning than at night. Maybe, I had just been really exhausted and not noticed.

A knock on my door had my eyes springing open. "Get out of bed little bitch." I nearly growled at Jed's voice but sat up. My back hurt like hell, the nerves raging against my treatment yesterday, but the wounds were sealed. I knew they were.

"Who the fuck is that?" A deep, so incredibly rich, voice asked. I nearly jumped out of my skin. I kept my mouth shut as I tumbled onto the floor in shock.

"Oh my," I whispered with confusion.

I had an Angel in my bed. It was the only explanation. His skin was a beautiful rich tone that was accented by his navy shirt and jeans. I couldn't understand how he was fitting in my bed, because this beautiful man was nearly a foot and a half taller than me. His gold eyes sparkled with amusement and rage, a very confusing combination. Maybe he was an avenging Angel? That made sense.

I reached forward with curiosity and touched his dark long hair that seemed to float down to his ribs. I was fascinated by the gold rings that lopped along his ear and the way he played with his small gold ring in his lip. Now this man was beautiful, there was no denying it. I mean, what were the chances that I'd be surrounded by so many beautiful men all the time? He smelled like sea salt, which reminded me of this place. I loved that.

"Who are you?" I blinked my eyes, leaning forward, and asked in sincere curiosity. His structured jawline had a trimmed beard that made me shiver slightly. I really liked how it looked on him.

The man flashed a set of perfect white teeth before saying, "Atlas."

I flushed in realization. "Oh, I thought you were an Angel. This is awkward."

Atlas chuckled softly before another bang on my door had me jumping into his arms. I wasn't positive why I had done it, but the soft rumbling of his chest had me relaxing. I didn't even mind the slight pain from his grip.

"Maya," Jed warned, "get your ass out of bed before I break-in."

Atlas let out a small growl, I slapped my hand on his mouth, "getting ready!"

"Bitch," Jed muttered before stomping off. I sighed and turned toward the massive man with a big grin.

"Did you stay the night?" I asked with curiosity.

He nodded cautiously. "I hope that's okay."

I flashed a smile and cupped his jaw. "That was my first sleepover ever. Thanks for that."

Atlas shook his head and smiled. "Angel, you are something else."

He then opened his dark tan jacket and handed me a white polo. I grinned and stood up, realizing I was only in underwear and a shirt. My blush alerted Atlas because he let out a low rumbling sound that had my skin breaking out in shivers. What was it about that damn noise?

"You should get dressed," he groaned before deflating into the bed. I nodded and briefly wondered why he looked so pained. I shimmied on my skirt before turning to take off my shirt. I grimaced at the pain in my back, despite superficial appearances.

I pulled on my bra and gently tugged the polo on before turning around. I gasped as Atlas looked down at me with frustration and anger. I whimpered at his imposing height, which caused him to lift me up under the thighs and bring me to eye level.

"Don't be afraid of me Maya," he whispered gently, no longer looking angry. "I would never hurt you, Angel."

I nodded, now that I was looking at him in the eye, I felt better. I knew I had no reason to fear him, but the man was truly massive.

"When I arrived yesterday, your back..." He growled quietly. My eyebrows shot up as I shook my head furiously. I so didn't want to talk about this.

"It was an old wound," I muttered quietly.

"That was actively bleeding and healing while I watched?" He growled again.

I raised my eyebrow. "You actually saw it heal? *Wow*. What was that like?"

He frowned and asked, "Have you always had healing abilities?"

I licked my lips, debating, and responded, "only when skin is broken."

His chest rumbled again as he demanded, "does that happen often?"

I flushed and tucked my head down into his shoulder. He sighed and brought a hand into my hair. "I will let this go for now Maya, but I expect an answer. The boys will also."

"No!" I whisper yelled.

He grunted, "we have to tell them."

"I don't want to worry the only friends I have, they will leave me!" I sounded panicked. Somehow their loss, after less than 24 hours, would devastate me.

Atlas's eyes darkened as he tried to reassure me, "no one will leave you Maya, but I have to tell Marco."

I whimpered as I spoke softly, "he's going to be mad."

Atlas scoffed. "Not at you Angel."

My alarm went off then as I scrambled to turn it off. My mother hated the noise. Atlas sighed before picking up my PJ shirt from the ground, I cringed at the blood on it. He tucked it into his jacket and leaned forward into my space.

"The twins are here with Henry. I expect to see you tonight at the house. If anything scares you between now and then, you will call me. Okay?"

I bit my lip and nodded, "I promise." *Could I call him just for fun?*

"Good." He nodded with a tense expression. I watched him leave my room and swayed briefly on my feet. Damn. Now Cosmo hadn't said anything about situations like that.

I grabbed my bag, tucked my phone in the bottom of it, and surfaced into the hall. The trailer was quiet and I made it nearly to the front door, before a meaty gross hand grasped my neck. I cringed at the feeling and waited for the scent of tobacco to disappear. It didn't.

"You think you can ignore me?" Jed whispered in a disgusted voice.

"I slept in," I mumbled quietly.

"Ignore me again and your door stays unlocked at night," he growled with yellow teeth. His hand bit into my neck as he pressed his disgusting body against mine. I whimpered, but it seemed to only encourage him.

"Jed Baby," my mother's voice called, "come back to bed."

I prayed he would. Jed grunted, squeezing my neck harder, before releasing me and walking away. I stumbled through the door and practically jogged toward the waiting SUV. I let my hair fall onto my neck and offered a weak, watery smile.

"What's wrong?" Ledger asked. Henry helped me into the back and gave me a sweet smile. It made my heart flutter nervously.

"Nothing," I mumbled.

Anani turned in his seat and looked me over with intense eyes, "your bruises are gone."

I shrugged, "maybe they weren't as bad as you thought."

Henry mumbled something before grasping my hand. The action made both of us blush as Ledger sighed and pulled onto the street. I don't think Henry blushed because he was embarrassed like I was though. The morning was a gloomy one and I couldn't seem to shake the feeling of sadness that invaded my bones. Once Atlas told them, they would think I was all messed up. They wouldn't want to be my friends anymore.

"Coffee?" Ledger asked while pulling through a green and white drive-through.

Henry and Anani ordered while I frowned at the menu. Ledger smiled, "you've never been to Starbucks?"

I leaned forward on my knees, over Henry, to peak at the menu. Henry made a low sound in his throat as the hand clasping mine moved to my hip. His hand was hot, but it steadied me. Anani turned in his seat to see the commotion and groaned. I looked back over my shoulder to find Ledger silently laughing.

"What?" I asked confused.

"What would you like to drink, Firefly?" Ledger mumbled with amusement.

"Something sweet please," I decided and sat back. Henry's hand gripped my waist gently as I settled against his warmth. Human contact felt great. Except, I wasn't positive they were humans. I mean, I didn't know what they were, but the dragon theory seemed valid. I sighed contently because I fit perfectly into Henry's side.

"We should get her some leggings," Anani muttered.

Ledger let out a loud laugh. "You don't mind the skirt on anyone else."

"I don't mind it on her, I mind anyone else seeing her in it," he shot back.

I raised a brow. "Why do I need leggings?"

Henry snorted quietly, "I'm sure Anani is just worried about you getting cold."

"Oh, that's sweet," I smiled, "don't worry though, I'll be okay."

Anani growled quietly as Ledger passed out our drinks. I took mine, a dark blended color, and sipped it. I made a sound of contentment at the sweetness that exploded within my mouth.

"Good?" Ledger tossed back a look.

"Amazing," I sighed and tapped Anani's shoulder while leaning forward.

He looked back and grinned at me. "Yes, Peanut ?"

"What does yours taste like?" *What? I was curious!*

He smirked as he said, "not as sweet as yours, I like my coffee bitter."

I frowned. "Why? Sweet things are the best."

Ledger snickered. "He knows that. It's just his metaphorical cold shower right now."

"Cold shower? Are you too hot?" I wondered out loud. "I'm sure you could take off your shirt if you are." Henry sputtered as Ledger started laughing a deep chuckle. "Yes Anani, why don't you take off your shirt?"

Anani tossed him a scowl before giving me a playful smile. "You want me to take off my shirt?"

"Of course," I rationalized, "you're hot."

Anani bit his lip, holding back a smile, "thanks, Peanut , I'll be sure to remember that."

I flushed at the heat in his eyes. Well, now I really wanted to see him without a shirt on. I wanted to trace those tattoos.

Ledger hit the back of his head. "Shut it, Casanova."

"Is that his real name?" I asked Henry. He racked his hand through his soft blonde curls with a head shake and small smile.

I continued, "that would be very neat if it was. Giacomo Girolamo Casanova is a very well known historic author from what I've read."

Henry flashed me a smile. "You know about Casanova?"

"I've read a lot," I noted. "Most of it about history, but you have to learn the past to understand the present."

Something sparked like a firework in his gray eyes as both boys up front groaned. "Now, you've done it, Firefly."

What?

"Come on," Henry whispered as the twins bickered. We were at school and quickly hopped out. I frowned and thought about how I would pay the twins back for my coffee.

"Henry?" I asked quietly, his hand still in mine. "Can you help me find a job?"

Henry's cheeks grew pink and a soft smile came onto his lips, "I'm sure we can find you something, but the boys don't think it's a good idea for you to work in town."

I frowned, "well why not?"

He chuckled softly, "they don't like the idea of our mate working."

"But you're all friends and half of you work," I reasoned.

Henry smiled softly, "I know Sweetheart, but just trust me on this. How about we find you something with Marco's company?"

I bit my lip gently. "Maybe. What if I find something I really want to do?"

His eyes crawled across my face and he smiled, "I don't think anyone would ever have an issue with you pursuing something you want to do, Maya. Just as long as you aren't doing it due to some misplaced notion that you need to pay us back."

I did need to pay them back though.

We continued to walk toward the school and were met by a large student body crowd. I cringed at the confined space and shuffled toward the side. The twins followed behind us as we made it to the lockers.

"Lil Henry getting his dick wet?" Lorn's voice echoed near us. Henry let out a sound that made my skin break out in shivers as both twins moved with ease toward us. What was this man's problem?

"Lorn." Henry's voice grew vacant and a cold chill flashed across his face, "didn't you learn your lesson yesterday?"

I looked up and was surprised to find Lorn had a bruised face. My mouth popped open as a sneer formed on his lips.

"Didn't you know, princess?" He growled as he continued, "your boyfriend's older brothers beat the shit out of me yesterday."

I flushed and felt my body tremor just slightly. I hated being the cause of violence. Something else sparked in my chest though, something very defensive about the way he was talking about, and to, Henry.

"Don't bring her into this," Anani snapped with his temper rising.

"Why?" Lorn grinned, "she is literally the reason for this."

I sunk into Ledger's chest as he wrapped an arm around my waist. Lorn snorted and shook his head, "so not just Henry, huh?"

A voice sounded from the end of the hallway causing all of us to pause. "Mr. Matchers, I do believe you are supposed to be in a meeting."

I found Marco strolling toward us, suit pressed clean to his body, and radiating power. Lorn scoffed and shook his head, "what do you know about my schedule?"

Those pale green eyes found mine with amusement as he answered, "a lot, considering I just had you benched for the next game."

"What the fuck?" Lorn thundered.

Marco grinned a predatory smile. "Harassment charges

could have resulted in something far worse. I'd take your luck where you can find it."

Lorn snarled, "fuck all of you. This whore isn't worth it."

I cringed at his harsh words as Marco snapped out a hand, closing around his neck. "Call her that ever again and the ending of last night will be vastly different."

With a distasteful sneer, Lorn jogged away after being released. Instantly, I relaxed and instead of being scared of how the men had acted, I felt comforted. Was that terrible? It felt nice to feel protected. Safe. Sheltered. I was always getting beat up on and now there were people who weren't allowing that. I would have to make sure to be as equally as good of a friend.

"Classroom now," Marco pointed to a door. I found his eyes hard and plastered to my face. I paled, knowing he had talked to Atlas.

The boys started to follow and Marco shook his head, "go to class. I need to talk to her alone first." My fight or flight instincts surfaced I flicked my eyes to the door because a very small part of me wanted to get the heck out of here.

Anani grunted and pulled me into a tight hug, "see you soon, Peanut ."

"Firefly," Ledger said in a lazy smooth tone.

Henry squeezed my hand and walked off with them. Marco's calculating smile was gone and replaced with anger. I flinched away from him as we moved into a classroom, his big hands locking the door.

"Maya," he whispered through a thick voice.

I squeaked, expecting the worst, as he turned. I was confused by the heartbreaking expression on his face as he picked me up into his arms. I felt my entire body relax against his. Oh. I had expected anger, not this. Then again, I always expected anger.

I mumbled, "I didn't want you to know, I didn't want to lose my new friends."

Marco grunted quietly, shaking his head, "you would never lose me as a friend Maya."

I pulled back and frowned, "you promise?"

Those green eyes sparkled slightly with darkness. "As long as you promise to tell me the truth."

I worried my lip and shook my head. "No, I have to protect you guys."

Marco sat down at the desk and pulled me to sit in front of him. My elevated position made him seem less scary. I was so small compared to him. I imagined I must look funny next to him and Atlas. I was like a tiny mouse next to a lion. *I want to be a flippin' lion.*

"I promise you, Maya," he whispered, running a hand over my jaw, "we can take care of ourselves."

I shook my head. "What type of friend would I be if I put you in trouble though? I'll be fine, Marco. I healed already."

He growled, "so who put the fucking bruises on your neck this morning?"

I paled. "No one."

"Liar," he snarled. I flinched and shrunk into the wood desk.

He cursed and sighed. "Please Maya."

He placed his head on my thigh and I tentatively reached out to run my hands through his silky dark hair. It was such a submissive position, it encouraged me to crawl into his lap. He looked up surprised, but wrapped me up quickly. I found I liked being wrapped up in his arms, it felt comforting and warm. It felt right.

"Maybe soon," I mumbled my compromise. "I don't want to lose you guys just yet."

"Atlas said your back was flogged and bleeding last night," he said through a strangled voice while pressing his lips to my temple. "Why didn't you call? How bad was it? I saw the shirt he brought back."

I swallowed. "I managed to get myself in bed. It'll be okay, Marco, I promise."

He shook his head and seemed to mutter the first part, "I'm not letting this go. But until tonight, let's just talk about your healing."

I flushed and looked down, "I'm a freak."

Marco hissed and brought two massive hands under my chin, "healing yourself is in your nature, you are not a freak."

I shook my head with tears filling my eyes, "my mother said the devil righted my body because I was a sinner."

A pair of warm hands soothed my back gently. "Honey, it is nothing like that at all. I can heal myself as well. I promise you, your mother is wrong."

I frowned, tears streaming, as I blinked, "you can heal?"

He nodded slowly. I offered a small sigh of confusion, well that didn't make sense. Marco wasn't evil. He was amazing.

"I promise to explain more tonight," Marco offered in a quiet voice before looking down at his watch, "you need to get your cute butt to class though."

I nodded, "okay, do you have work today?"

He flashed me a grin. "Why? Want me to stay at school with you?"

My face flamed pink as I stammered, "always nice to have friends around."

Marco smiled brilliantly. "I wish I could stay, honey. Unfortunately I'm a tad old for high school."

I pursed my lips thoughtfully and asked, "How old are you?"

He rose a brow with a soft smile. "24."

My lips popped into a small circle. "Well that's okay. I'm almost 18."

He chuckled a soft, enticing sound. "Are you worried about our age difference?"

"Well I don't want you to think of me as a kid," I muttered. No one wanted to be friends with a kid.

Marco chuckled before smoothing my hair back. "You don't have to worry about that, beautiful. You may be new to all of this, but I see you."

The small butterflies in my stomach fluttered nervously. I wasn't familiar with this feeling, but it encouraged me to curl further into Marco. He obliged and held me close as my nose trailed along his neck. A soft, low sound echoed through his chest.

"Alright," he sighed after a peaceful few minutes. "I need to get you to class before I decide to implement a mandatory skip day."

I rolled my head against his shoulder to look up at him, "that doesn't sound terrible." My face was slightly pink and I could feel myself absorbing his affection like a starving kitten. It didn't help that our position was rather intimate, my body and head wedged on his lap and shoulder. It was a comfortable and warm position.

"Are you flirting with me, Maya?" Marco cooed softly while picking up a piece of my hair and twirling it gently between his tanned fingers. Our noses were so close to one another and I wasn't positive why, but I felt like if I just leaned up and pressed my lips to his, it would feel amazing.

I'd never had my first kiss but somehow I knew a kiss between Marco and I would be special.

I sat up with raised eyebrows. "Was I? I've never flirted with anyone before."

Marco's head fell back as a deep chuckle filled the air. "Gods Maya, you are a breath of fresh air. I have never met someone with as much curiosity as you."

I flushed. "I have a lot of years to make up for."

"Well, it seems you have six dragons willing to aid in that endeavor," he chuckled.

I smiled and asked, "if you're dragons, do I get to be the princess?"

Marco's teeth flashed white in a dangerous smile. "Didn't the dragons eat the princess?"

I blush at his tone and reached for a response, "fine, I'll be a dragon then, or a knight."

He hummed appreciatively after a dark chuckle. "We will create a brand new character for you, Maya. I promise."

His eyes softened as he lifted a tanned hand to my cheek and smoothed it gently with a thoughtful look. I leaned into it and practically purred before he wrapped me into a hug again. I waited for him to let go but with the way my head was tucked under his chin, I wasn't positive that would happen.

"Marco?" I whispered, loving his name on my tongue.

"Hm?" He offered a distracted sound.

"You told me to go to class but won't let me go," I whispered with a slight smile.

He looked down and chuckled, brushing my chin in a soft hold. "Sorry, Maya."

As he walked me out the door, I offered him a slight hand squeeze and moved down the hall. I slipped into my first class and found my space open between my three friends. Anani squeezed my hip in passing as Ledger tilted his head back so that his messy curls fell back. Henry offered me a smile that had my face lighting up with a blush. He made me feel all warm and fuzzy, that Henry.

These feelings were really worrying me.

I would have to watch out, I didn't want to burden them with my emotions. Of course, I was going to feel affection toward them, but they didn't need to know the extent. I was too much of a weirdo as it was.

5

HENRY

I went to lunch today.

My computer lab didn't hold nearly the same appeal as our little mate now. I watched her with an obsessive interest as she ate a sandwich from a lavender cooler bag that Ledger had picked out. Without thinking about it, Anani had handed her over some sharpies and she'd begun to draw a beautiful set of flowers. God, she was just so... so Maya.

I watched her golden eyes flash through the magazine she'd found at the library. Vogue? I frowned. It wasn't that I disagreed with the magazine, but she could do much better than that. I had already concluded that Maya had a very alternative upbringing and she was essentially a fresh face in this rather stark world. I felt bad for enjoying that fresh innocence. It radiated off her like sunlight in a darkened cell. It was intoxicating. Her light and hope. She was obviously very smart. But also had this whimsical, almost childlike curiosity to her. Something I wanted to protect. Honestly, I just wanted to protect her. Every single inch of that golden skin.

Mine.

Well, at least that was what my dragon thought. What he obsessed about. God I wish I was better than that, but I was not. At all.

My research had found very little on Maya and even less about her history. It hadn't been difficult to arrange for her personal identification, but it seemed as of right now she didn't have a Social Security number. She essentially didn't exist. I think Marco loved and hated that.

On one hand, it was far easier to protect her without a paper trail in Earth realm. On the other, it meant something terrible had happened to have her life twisted as such. My lips pulled back in a light snarl as a few football players walked by, all looking at Maya.

Maya, who had no idea how beautiful she was. Maya, who had no idea that she was simply intoxicating and sexy without trying. *Maya.*

Shit. This was bad.

My dragon snarled under the surface of my skin and before I knew it, I had grabbed her hand within mine. I felt awkward a bit after they'd passed because my fucking instinctual reaction was very different than how I normally interacted with humanity. It wasn't that I hadn't known this side of me existed. I was a fucking beta. I just hadn't found a need for it to be so damn prominent until her. Now I felt a range of things that I hadn't expected to feel regarding her, all of them insanely protective and terrible territorial. Maya looked up through her lashes and offered me a smile that showcased her flushed golden cheekbones.

As the twins continued to talk about something relatively unimportant, I studied her. Intensely. How was someone who was so small and beautiful possible? Maybe she wasn't real? I squeezed her hand to ensure that she was right here. I noticed she had placed down her sandwich and was frowning down at the table in introspection.

"What's wrong?" I asked her.

She met my eyes and nibbled her lip nervously. "Henry, do most friends act like this?" I could see the gears turning in her head and this small flame that had lit up behind those golden eyes. I needed to figure out what type of fucking shifter she was. Like yesterday.

It wasn't completely my fault I kept getting distracted. You try to keep focused when your mate crawls over your lap first thing in the morning in a tiny skirt. I had to grip her hip ridiculously hard just to avoid running it along the silky skin of her leg and ass.

"Act like what?" I couldn't help but smile because I knew she was probably feeling the mate bond. We had no idea how it would affect her since I had yet to determine what she was exactly.

She nodded toward our hands, "I don't think that this is how friends act. But I don't care. I should care. Plus I feel…"

I was around the table before I could rationalize my action as I turned Maya towards me gently. I cupped her jaw, "how do you feel Sweetheart?" Honestly, I wasn't even going to blame this on my dragon anymore. Although, the fucker was laughing at me.

Maya's plush lip was being tortured as I tried to not stare at it. Instead of doing what I wanted to, which was nibbling on it myself and then soothing it with my tongue, I simply watched her.

Fuck, Henry. Get a fucking grip. My dragon offered a huff as if he was annoyed at my attempt for control.

I could tell she was about to respond, but then Malloy reached our table. Instead of moving, I tucked her more solidly under my arm and buried my nose in her hair. "We will talk about this later, okay?"

Her brow dipped and she shook her head, "I don't want you guys to get hurt."

There was her protective nature again. Part of me was immensely turned on by it and the other part was terrified about her need for that amount of concern. I knew something had happened last night because Marco had said we needed to talk privately. Atlas had found out something regarding Maya, and my guess was that it wasn't good.

My chest hurt thinking about her being in danger. Maya didn't know it yet, but her time in that goddamn trailer was at an end. She had officially four school days until she turned eighteen. Friday at midnight I was dragging her ass out of there. She didn't have to stay with us, I'd put her up wherever she wanted, but I didn't want her around Jed. Jed who had been arrested for drug trafficking and suspected sex trafficking. Somehow the fucker had gotten off and my suspicion was that he had connections in the human world to aid with influencing the system.

"Hey Sugar," Malloy winked while sitting across from us, "why the long face?"

I was able to keep my reaction to a minimum as Maya scowled, "I don't have a long face, it's perfectly shaped."

Anani chuckled as Ledger shook his head. Malloy tilted his head and grinned, "you're an odd one, aren't you?"

"Maybe you're the odd one," she retorted, looking amused.

He snorted and nodded, "agreed, Maya."

I felt jealous over their fucking interaction. The fact that I was nearly positive Malloy wasn't even fucking attracted to women didn't matter to my dragon. Possessive bastard. I tried to ignore it as a low rumble came from my chest and Malloy frowned at me. I kept my face neutral because this really did not need to turn into what happened with Lorn earlier. I'm surprised Maya didn't lose it and run. Instead, she leaned her head against my chest and her eyes fluttered just slightly. My lips curled because I'd realized yesterday that the sound coming from my dragon actually relaxed her. It had been the same way she'd reacted to Marco. It didn't surprise me completely because while Marco was alpha, I was his beta, so we would be the first two she'd feel the strongest attraction to.

Before anything else could be said, an odd sensation came over me. I frowned as I looked behind Malloy and realized who exactly was walking over. Shit. This could only go bad.

"Maya Sweetheart," I murmured as she peaked up at me. I heard the twins still as they watched evil itself walk its way across the cafeteria.

"Yeah?" She asked sincerely.

"I want you to remember that whatever happens next, I am not involved with anyone. I am only focused on our... friendship. Okay? It's just the boys and you. Alright?"

This was such a fucked-up situation.

Her eyes examined my expression and she probably didn't even realize that she was using her energy to search me for lies. She smiled right as a shadow of deranged awfulness covered the table.

"Hey boys," a high pitched scratchy voice sounded.

Fucking Becky Ash.

6
MAYA

I looked up at the shadow covering our table and my eyes widened. She was so freaking pretty. *Holy crap.* When she looked at me next to Henry, her face turned violent and I found my heart racing. That menace and deranged violence reminded me of my mom.

"Henry Sweetheart." She leaned forward as her blouse opened and my eyes flashed to her… holy crap those can't be real. Who is this lady? She had the body of a thirty-year-old and her face was very smooth. Like a doll. Her hair was a weird white color that was dark at the roots. I had to admit, I was confused about her, but she was beautiful in a very unique way. Why didn't my body look like that? Was it wrong I was a bit jealous?

"Is this your new foster sister?" She asked curiously in a harsh voice, "she looks so little. What are you kid, like fourteen?"

Before I could stop myself, a snarl built in my throat at the way she was treating me. Ledger covered it with a cough but I turned my body so I was shielding my boys from her. Even Malloy was temporarily included. He was a goofy guy but I was starting to think we could be friends... just not the same type of friend I was with the other boys. I was getting really frustrated with not having a word to describe how I was feeling.

"I'm sorry, I didn't catch your name," I stated keeping my eyes and expression neutral.

Her face darkened, "that's because I didn't give it to you."

"Well," I frowned, "that is a bit rude, isn't it? I get it though, maybe manners aren't your thing or you didn't learn proper introductions? Whatever the case, I'm Maya."

I put out my hand and the woman's face turned red.

Still, no introduction, but Henry was silently shaking next to me.

"Henry," she growled, "Sweetheart, are we going out tonight? My parents aren't home so if you want to come over... the twins can join also, my friends don't have plans."

My lips pressed as a growl bubbled up. She couldn't be their friends. They were mine.

Henry sighed and pressed a kiss to my forehead, "I'm not free tonight, Becky."

So her name was Becky?

"With work?" She narrowed her eyes at me. I wondered what he would say.

"No." He massaged my scalp gently. "The lot of us are busy every night for the foreseeable future."

My skin shivered as I leaned back into him. Becky offered me a glare, before something flashed in her eyes, and walked away. Wow, her skirt was way shorter than mine. It was sort of impressive. I sighed and looked back at Henry, his eyes warm on my face as Malloy looked over the four of us.

"Thanks, Peanut ," Anani winked, "you looked like you were going to tear off her head."

"Sounds messy," I mumbled softly.

"Firefly," Ledger looked at my sandwich, "eat up."

Malloy spoke and rose a brow with honest curiosity, "so I have to ask Maya, are you single?"

I jumped as a ripple of growls and low chest noises had Malloy swearing. Poor guy. He put his hands up, "alright fine. Nevermind. I'm just going to assume she's with all of you."

"Good assumption," Anani bit out.

"So being single?" I frowned and asked Henry, "what does that mean exactly?"

The bell rang as Malloy frowned and all my guys made an excuse to stand up. I smiled as Ledger helped me up and the other two walked behind us slowly. I looked up at the orange-tipped hair of my friend. Today he wore a comfy hoodie and on the front was a bright neon design.

"Ledger?" I asked softly, "could I get a hoodie like yours?"

He flashed me a beautiful smile that had me smiling in return, "do you want it right now, Firefly?"

My lips pressed together trying to suppress my hope. "But then you will be cold."

Ledger stopped and my throat went dry as he tugged his hoodie up and the polo underneath rode up. I made a panicked sound because my body reacted, heating to the sight of his smooth muscular abdomen. He had tattoos as well. I wanted to see those.

"Maya?" He asked handing me the sweatshirt and snapping my eyes up.

I blushed at being caught looking at how beautiful he was. "Thanks."

He helped me tug it on and once it was over he leaned closer against my ear to whisper, "never be embarrassed for looking at me, Maya. I'm always looking at you."

Oh.

I really needed to find out the difference between friends and liking one another. This was getting confusing. I considered them friends, but there was this pulsating in my chest that told me they were so much more.

I couldn't think about that though. I just had to make it to Friday night at midnight.

"I'm going to go use the washroom," I said breathlessly and walked over to a door, practically closing myself in it. My heart was beating so fast. What was going on?

"Hey." The red-haired girl from my first class stood in front of the mirror. "You're Maya right?"

I nodded and pressed my hands against the counter trying to regulate my breathing slightly. If she noticed, she didn't comment. Instead, she hopped up onto the counter and offered me a grin, "I'm Jordan McFury."

"Nice to meet you," I smiled softly. The woman was taller than me and wispy in stature. I could see a soft kindness radiating from her deep green eyes and it comforted me. I was terrible around women because of my mom, they made me nervous. Not her though. She seemed nice.

"I'm so sorry you had to deal with Becky," she groaned. "She is the worst. Absolutely awful. You seemed to hold your own though."

"She really didn't like me," I stated with a slight frown.

"That's because you are with them." She nodded as if motioning to my boys outside. "She's been gunning for one of them since freshman year and now you are here less than two days and those boys are all over you. Actually, it's worse than that, they are like straight-up obsessed with you. I mean that is probably dramatic, but also maybe not because they have been warning everyone off. I mean, of course, we've all heard how possessive dragons can be about their mates, but man, I don't think any of us actually considered how bad it would be."

"What do you mean 'gunning for them'?" I didn't like her doing anything in reference to them. It didn't bother me as much when Jordan talked about them, but not Becky.

She kicked her legs while sitting forward. "So you know Marco, right? The older one."

I blushed and her eyes popped open.

"It *is* all of them, isn't it?" She grinned and clapped. "Shifter society is so much easier to deal with."

"Shifter society?" I tilted my head.

"Oh, don't act so naive." She chuckled. "I'm a wolf shifter. Half this school is part of one shifter community or another. For example, that asshole Lorn is an alpha for a small bear pack ten miles from here…"

Okay, I would totally ask about shifters later. I wasn't focused on that though.

"So what about Marco?"

"Well, they are rich. I mean, you probably know," she exclaimed dramatically, "like I mean really fucking rich. Like his company is worth billions. *Billions!*"

"Wow," I whispered, "I didn't know that."

"But she has gone after each of them," Jordan continued with enthusiasm. "She's the worst, besides Lorn. My pack is pretty cool though, I mean my dad is alpha so if it wasn't, I would be pissed. You will have to come to our pack lands sometime. Wolf shifters can be a bit aggressive, but most of us are okay. Plus my dad loves Marco, so I can't imagine it will be an issue to arrange."

"Sounds cool," I flashed a smile. *How else was I*

supposed to react to what she was saying? Also, Jordan didn't seem aggressive at all, but maybe she was different than the others in her pack? Wait, was she saying she was part of a pack of wolves?

"Oh, another question," she bubbled out and I realized I was completely relaxed because of her excitement, "is your voice naturally like that?"

"Yeah," I muttered suddenly feeling uncomfortable, "I had an injury a bit ago."

"That is so cool," she exclaimed. "I mean not that the injury, but it sounds so unique."

The warning bell rang as she hopped up and hooked arms with me as she led me towards the bathroom door into the large hallway across from our classroom. "Here give me your phone."

I handed it to her and she typed in a number quick, kissed my cheek, and waltzed into the classroom. I blinked a couple of times and sighed. *Well damn.* I scowled at swearing, I didn't want to be like my mom.

"Maya," Ledger snagged me gently into his arms. I blushed as the eyes of students still waiting in the hallway bore into us, so I turned into his warm chest. His hand came under my chin.

I noted softly, "I just met Jordan."

"That's good," He flashed a smile before his expression turned serious, "but I need to apologize."

I frowned, "why?"

"I didn't mean to make you uncomfortable earlier, Firefly," he whispered. "I would never try to embarrass you or make you feel bad."

I pressed my lips together but my words came out anyway, "I wasn't embarrassed, I just couldn't think around you, my heart was beating super fast."

A warmth spilled into his eyes as he tilted his head, "so you *were* looking at me."

Something occurred to me and I spoke freely, trying to distract myself from the butterflies, "Jordan said some things and I'm a bit confused. She said she was the daughter of an alpha and part of these 'shifter communities.' She said Lorn was a bear and that Becky was 'gunning for you guys' because you're rich. What does she mean by all that? And after hanging out with Jordan, I really don't think the group of us are acting like friends. I'm just confused-"

"Maya," Ledger put a thumb on my lips, "breathe."

I inhaled and nodded before he answered, "for now, let's wait on the shifter aspect until home, okay?"

I nodded.

"As for the friend thing, you're right. Friends don't act like us."

I knew we would be late to class, but I leaned into him for comfort anyway as I asked, "how are we different? Why?"

Ledger swallowed while worrying his lip, "I think we should talk about this later. Just know that most people don't act like this with their friends."

"So this isn't how I should act toward all my friends?" I rose a brow.

"Absolutely not," Anani growled softly from behind me. I jumped a little, but his large warm hands smoothed my waist. My ribs were still tender, but honestly, it wasn't terrible and his hands made it feel better. Those embers grew hotter inside of my stomach. Why did I only feel like this around them? It was like my chest was warming and a voice inside of me was humming happily.

"Huh?" I asked confused. "So how do I know then?"

Henry chuckled, walking forward with his hands in his

pockets. "Yes Anani, how does she know who gets this special treatment?"

Ledger smoothed my hair thoughtfully, "only us six, Firefly."

Anani nodded. "Yeah Peanut , just us six."

Henry frowned. "But you can make more friends, Sweetheart."

Ledger grunted at the same time Anani made a distressed sound. Henry rolled his eyes and tugged me into his side. "Don't listen to them, you can be friends with whoever you want. Just," he hesitated, "maybe keep touching them to a minimum."

I nodded and admitted, "I don't really like touching other people, but it's different with you guys. Plus, I sincerely doubt anyone else will want to be friends with me. Don't worry."

We walked into the door late as Henry made a concerned noise. I wasn't positive what it was in reaction to.

"Class has started, please be seated." Our professor raised a dark brow. The four of us scuttled to sit down as I found myself wedged between the twins once more. I shivered under the coolness of the window that was thrown open. A damp wind pushed through the room with a vigor that reminded me of my nights in the basement.

"Sinner." *Hit 1 from father*.

"You kneel on the floor because you're a sinner."

"Sinner." *Hit 2 from mother*. "Beat the devil from you."

"Sinner." *Hit 3, father again*. "On the floor like the beast you are."

"Sinner." *Hit 4, mother again*.

"Maya," Ledger whispered with concern. His hands wrapped around my trembling ones as my eyes refocused back on the class. I could feel a cool wetness against my cheek that confused me. I moved my hand up to brush away the offensive moisture.

I blinked to refocus in the class. I tried to ignore the three intense stares and focus on the task at hand. I didn't want them to know how broken I was. When I was alone, no one was around to see me cry. No one was around to see the freak I was. The absolute devil I was. For once, no matter how temporary, they made me feel wanted, and I was in no hurry to lose that.

"What the hell happened in there?" Anani whispered while we moved towards the gym. I swallowed and shook my head. Jordan tossed me a wave and I was starting to feel lucky that I had made a real friend, just in case the boys didn't want me.

My lip tilted down without permission.

"Maya." Ledger attempted to grab my hand.

"I'm fine," I crossed my arms tight enough to hold myself together, "really. Just a bad memory."

"What caused it?" Henry asked quietly, his warm hand touching my back gently.

I shook my head trying to gather myself. "Let's focus on gym, okay?"

I heard three dissatisfied sounds, then Ledger muttered, "fine."

Except as the twins entered the locker room, I was gently tugged back by Henry. His eyes were swirling with a dark shade and this warm shiver crawled across my skin from the energy that circulated around us. He spoke quietly, "you can't keep saying you don't want to talk about it, Maya."

I licked my lips and shrugged, "it was just a bad memory, what is there to talk about?"

Henry's eyes darkened as he kissed my forehead and

nodded toward the locker room. He was right. Friends didn't keep secrets and I was keeping a lot of them.

Once in the locker room, I changed and tied up my sneakers. I looked down at the second-hand shoes and wondered how I would even go about getting a job. There were so many things I didn't understand and it felt like I had no time to catch up.

The boys were waiting for me and I almost confronted them about the friendship thing, but when Anani grasped my hand and pulled me toward the class, I just couldn't. I should have told him to stop. I didn't want to though. I didn't want to tell him that no one could ever be anything other than my friend. They deserved to know though. They deserved better. I was selfish though.

I really did have a devil inside me.

7
SAI

"This is fucked up, Marco," I hissed as I paced back and forth in the bastard's office. He worked from home most days and today was no exception. It was also due to the work being done in our seventh bedroom because everyone agreed Maya should have her own space.

That trailer thing wasn't going to last.

Dragons were protective and possessive by nature, so her situation was like chewing nails for us. I swallowed as he looked over her lack of history and the situation at hand.

"She has four days," Marco grunted. "We can't take her away before that."

"Her back was flogged!" I yelled as Atlas winced.

Marco's eyes flashed darkly as his dragon forced out a snarl at my outburst. I felt mine give a huff at his dominance before I threw myself down into a chair. This was fucking stupid.

"We just need to keep her here as much as possible," Marco murmured after a deep breath, "I don't want her to live there either, but until she is eighteen, we can't do anything. I don't think her mom would push anything legally but I would rather not risk it."

"How do we even know that is her birthday?" I growled.

Atlas sighed, "we don't. When she turns eighteen she will realize who her mates are, which is convenient for the group of us, but will probably really freak her out. I don't even want to think about what the hell we are going to do about the mating heat..."

Marco put his head down, "I didn't even think about that. We need to figure out what she is. Do either of you have any leads?"

Of course, we fucking didn't.

My entire body stilled as the door downstairs closed and voice rose up. Without a second thought, I was moving down the stairs to see Maya. It was difficult to control myself around her and it didn't help when she flashed me a brilliant smile.

"How was your day?" I asked her before grasping her jaw gently.

"Good," she chirped while leaning into me, "very good. Oh! My friend Jordan mentioned something though and the twins refuse to explain. Henry went all quiet and so I've been throwing out theories the entire drive from school."

Henry shook his head and threw himself down on the couch as the twins went towards the kitchen. Marco was next to me and pressing a kiss to the top of her head before offering me a look at what clearly was curiosity and amusement. What was she asking that made them so damn uncomfortable?

"What was the question?" Marco asked lightly.

Before either of us could respond, Atlas made his way downstairs and Maya offered a massive smile, slipping between us. Now, it goes without saying that Atlas is scary.

Legitimately terrifying, so when Maya all but threw herself in his arms, it had both Marco and me pausing.

He picked her up so she was sitting right on his crossed forearms before tossing us a wink. *Bastard.* I followed after as Marco stole her away and we sat down on the couch, Maya's slight form tucked against him. My hands twitched to hold her, but there was no getting her away from Marco right now.

"Maya was told by Jordan McFury about shifters in passing, she would like to know more," Henry drawled looking amused and stressed. My lip twitched because I could tell this entire situation, the chaos of it, bothered him. I liked messing with Henry a bit, I couldn't lie.

Marco made a low sound and twisted Maya so she was facing everyone, leaning against the sofa's armrest. My eyes flickered down to her long lean legs. Don't get me wrong, I knew in the human world 18 was an important age, but I can tell you as a 19-year-old dragon, I didn't give a fuck. So I didn't feel bad about appreciating how fucking gorgeous the woman was. Plus, if we wanted to go by legal standards, Washington's age of consent was 16.

I did scowl at Ledger's hoodie she was wearing, I have better sweaters than that.

"What do you want to know about shifters?" Marco asked looking genuinely confused about where to start.

She frowned and then grinned, "well what type of shifters are you? Better yet, what's a shifter? Why did Jordan say she was a wolf? I mean, do you just pick which animal you like and pretend to be it? If so I'm totally gunning for a house cat. I looked up the phrase and everything, it means *I'm aiming for it or trying to get it.*"

Anani burst out laughing and Henry threw himself back, muttering a curse.

"Gunning?" Atlas asked amused.

"Jordan said Becky Ash was gunning for you all," she chirped. "I mean, I don't want to be mean but she seemed very rude. I'm not a fan."

I shook my head as Marco seemed to rationalize what she was saying. Fucking Becky Ash.

"Henry?" Marco rose a brow.

"I explained that none of us have friendships outside of Maya," Henry conceded, his hands tapping on the leather arm chair. I was bouncing slightly with energy because I was really interested to see how Marco was going to manage to explain all this. I never denied that I wasn't a fucking instigator.

"How about we explain what shifters are first?" Ledger noted as Marco nodded.

"Alright," Marco stated, looking at Maya, "remember our conversation about dragons earlier?"

She nodded, "yeah about dragons eating princesses."

Oh holy hell.

"Christ Marco," Henry bit out. I didn't blame him, now all I could imagine was spreading her legs apart and showing her just how well dragons can eat princesses.

Marco chuckled and pressed his head down on Maya's collar bone, "yes, honey, that conversation. Well, unlike your mom and Jed, some people on Earth have the ability to turn into certain animals. The six of us turn into dragons."

My lips pressed together as Maya's magic, unintentionally, surrounded Marco searching for lies before her cheeks flushed. "Really?"

"Really..."

"Prove it," she chirped, her eyes filled with a live wire. Why hadn't we considered this?

"We would have to go outside..." Atlas didn't finish

because Maya was up and heading towards the back door. I didn't blame her. I would want to see it as well.

"Who is going to shift?" Anani asked quietly.

"I've got it," I responded as hot energy flashed through me. My dragon was way too fucking excited to show off. I pulled off my white polo as I took a moment to appreciate how stunning our little mate was, her eyes darkening upon seeing me as her cheeks turned bright red. I fucking loved that blush. I wanted to see that color all over her body.

I would also like to see her in a jacket. It was cold out.

"You sure?" I asked her as she bounced on her toes slightly, nodding bravely.

I stepped back and with ease, I shifted.

8
MAYA

Oh, sweet Christ.

"Oh. My. God," I muttered at the truly massive, crimson, dragon in front of me. I tried to categorize every feature from the thick armor-like scales to the wingspan that hit the entire width of the house. A pair of dark eyes watched me from above as I stepped forward because I needed to see this as close as possible. Experience this completely.

"Maya," Marco warned. I waved him off as the dragon in front of me snorted.

"This is so cool," I let out a laugh. I mean I knew these men were spectacular, so it shouldn't surprise me that they were more than just humans. After all, where else did all those fairytales come from?

Sai's massive head lowered so that his gaze was eye level with mine, his chin resting on the ground. I was shaking slightly, but mostly because of excitement, as I reached forward and shivered at the heat emanating from his scales. Something inside of my chest fluttered restlessly and it forced me closer until I had my face pressed against the massive snout.

"Do you fly?" I asked quietly as the world zeroed in on just this massive creature and me.

Sai snorted as if amused once again, the action causing my clothing to ruffle, as he nodded. "That is so cool," I murmured. "Can you take me up sometime?"

Something lit in his gaze as a deadly tail wrapped around my waist and lifted me up to his back with ease. I grinned and lodged myself right against his neck. That's when I realized Marco and Henry were talking.

"Sai no," Marco stated quietly.

"I get it," Henry stated his voice tense, "but you can't take her up, she doesn't even know how to hold on properly."

"I do too!" I scowled. "I'm fine Sai, really. Bunch of *negative nancies*." I came across that phrase as well while online. You can't even imagine all the fun stuff your phone can find.

Some of the stuff was a bit more confusing than others. For example, I was trying to figure out if it was normal for Atlas and I to sleep in the same bed. So I typed in 'friends who sleep together' and let me tell you, Atlas and I were not doing what they were. I had exited out of the site so fast, I'd nearly dropped my phone.

I had to admit... I sort of wanted to look it up again. It seemed like something I didn't know enough about.

The dragon underneath me let out a rumbling snicker at my words as I grinned. I inhaled and then we took off. I let out an excited cry as his magic surrounded me, something I hadn't had a name for before, and held me to his form. My eyes closed as the cool wind whipped past me and a feeling of euphoria settled over me. Something about heights really did it for me.

The entire coast line opened up for us and while we stayed in cloud cover, I felt absolutely free and uninhibited. I could feel something inside of me beating very fast and I was almost jealous that I was so clearly human.

While my ears were cold, his magic was keeping the rest of me warm and I had no idea how long we flew before the sky began to darken. Sai took us down with ease, I realized we'd gone up and down the coast, coming back to land right in the backyard. I let out a laugh as we landed and before I had time to prepare, the dragon under me disappeared. I let out a squeak as a pair of muscular arms caught me and I looked up at Sai.

"That was amazing," I whispered my smile large and authentic.

Sai's eyes were heated with something as he pressed his nose to mine and rubbed gently. "Yes, you are."

Huh?

"Christ Sai," Anani bit out, "get dressed."

My eyes immediately took greedy attention of his chest that was dark and colored in with these stunning gold patterns. I let my hand trace across it as a soft hum came from my throat. I frowned as I got plucked from his arms by Ledger as he explained, "bad idea, Firefly. Sai is on edge right now."

I frowned, looking at his serene face, but those eyes were dark and I almost felt like I could see his dragon looking back at me. When he spoke, it was nearly tri-layered, "she seemed to be just fine to me, Ledger."

I nibbled my lip, but froze when we got far enough away and I realized he was naked. My mouth popped open because *holy crap,* it was huge. Sai barked out a laugh as I squeaked and Ledger covered my eyes with a shake of his head. I couldn't help but want to look again. I mean, how did something so hard and large exist *there*? Had I just missed it? I mean, I would have noticed that before, no doubt. A warmth spread through me as we entered the house and Ledger muttered a curse.

"Please, someone take her before I do something dangerous," he grinds out as my feet landed and immediately, Marco had me wrapped up. He muttered a curse, but kept his head against my neck while breathing in.

"Henry," Marco bit out, "Tell Sai I expect to see him in my office later."

"Worth it!" Sai called out in passing. I totally tried to see if he was still naked. Marco stilled my head from turning as I offered him a wide-eyed expression. What? Then something occurred to me and I tried my damn best to not look down.

So that was what the equivalent of physically hitting on me looked like without clothes? I sort of really liked that. Was it bad I wanted to touch it? I didn't know if that was a thing. See? I really needed to talk to Jordan more, she could just bubble out those answers.

"Don't give me that look, honey," Marco drawled.

"What look?" I asked, my voice coming out different than I expected.

"Fucking shit," He muttered and then lifted me up, walking towards the couch because clearly, they'd forgotten I can walk. This time we went down a set of stairs to a movie room where I nearly crawled into the soft cushioning and sighed in relief. I loved soft fluffy things.

Atlas was stretched out and he motioned over to me as I crawled forward. Marco had distanced himself, and Henry and the twins were looking like they were in pain. No idea why. I smiled as Atlas lifted me into his arms and I wiggled in his lap getting comfortable. He chuckled. "Gentleman, this is nearly disappointing."

"Oh yeah?" Anani bit out. "You have no idea Atlas, no fucking idea."

"I do," he drawled as I hummed out a soft song. "I slept next to her all night."

"It was awesome," I nodded, "you should sleep next to me every night." Was this a good time to tell him that the internet said we should be doing other things during our sleepover as well? I needed someone to freakin' tell me if that was normal or not.

Henry barked out a laugh as Atlas's eyes grew dangerously sharp. Marco came to sit next to him and pinned me with a look as I tried to consider what was odd about what I'd just said. Nothing was the answer.

"Oh!" I just remembered, "so shifters. If you can turn into dragons, does Jordan turn into a wolf?"

"Yes," Marco nodded. Interesting.

"I'm jealous," I announced with a head nod, "I'm a boring human, and you are dragons."

"Well, about that," Henry notes, "I don't think you are just human."

I raised a brow and replied, "Henry, I feel like I would have known if I could turn into a dragon."

The twins chuckled softly at what I'd said as Sai returned. My eyes eagerly ran over his body as I tried to not look at his erection. That was what Cosmo had called it! An erection. I should ask them if that was the right term. Wait. I think they'd also referred to it as a *hard-on*. Huh. Well, now that I'd seen it that made a hell of a lot more sense. I couldn't confirm it was hard for sure until I touched it of course, but it made sense.

"I don't think you are a dragon," Marco noted softly. "I think you are something far more unique than that."

I let out a small laugh. "Marco, you're a flippin' dragon. That's pretty unique."

He tossed me a cocky smile that had me blushing. Then Ledger said something confusing me, "is it wrong that I want to hear her swear?"

"Yes," Henry scolded.

"I can swear," I pointed out.

Sai's eyes lit up, "yeah? Do it."

"You don't have to," Atlas stated.

"I want to hear it," Anani encourage.

I nibbled my lip and thought of what my mom would always say to Jed. "What do you want me to fucking say?" I squeaked at the end because it sounded so harsh and mean.

Sai burst out laughing as the twins just watched me in shock. Atlas sighed, "I don't even want to examine why I found that attractive."

"It was the *fucking* element," Henry noted.

Marco hummed, "it's true."

"What about fucking?" I frowned now just curious. I mean I knew what 'fucking' was. My mom used a bunch of slang that differed from the anatomy books I read.

"Do you know what fucking is?" Sai asked looking like he was on cloud nine.

"I mean, of course," I frowned, "I had the whole birds and the bees conversation. My mom used a bunch of different words than what the anatomy book had. Like she used the words 'fucking, dick, cock'..."

My mouth was covered by Marco as the twins laughed harder and Sai moved forward, crouching in front of me. He took my hand and spoke with a huge smile, "Maya, you are the most perfect creature on this entire planet, did you know that?"

Huh?

Atlas was hard underneath me and Marco was just staring into my gaze in an intimately intense way. Henry was muttering curses to himself. I opened my mouth to ask Marco to remove his hand from my mouth when a knock sounded on the door. All seven of us freezing, Marco removed his hand.

"Go get the door Sai," Marco muttered and helped me up off the couch.

"You know its the police right?" Sai stated softly.

"I'm aware, her mother and Jed must have called." Oh no. "I need to talk to her for a moment, please go delay them."

My heart was strung up tight. "I'm sorry." I knew the police were not a good sign.

Marco shook his head and looked down at me. "No worries, honey. I need you to be honest with me, alright?"

I nodded.

"Is your house safe for the night? If I let you walk out of here, will you be okay?"

Oh, I hated lying. I swallowed, "I think so."

He growled softly and shook his head. "You turn 18 this Saturday right?"

I nodded my head and he spoke quickly and quietly, "I don't want you staying in that place a moment longer than you have to. I want you to come to stay with us. Are you comfortable with that?"

Was I? I flicked my eyes around the room and the feeling in my chest grew warmer. I nodded and spoke softly, "yes. Yes, I'm okay with that."

Marco flashed me a brilliantly white smile right as two

men in dark uniforms rounded the corner. "Mr. Moretti, so sorry to interrupt here, we were just sent to check on a girl from the twin's school. A few students saw her leaving with them today, so we figured we would check here first." *This didn't sound like my mom. This sounded like Jed.*

I knew they saw Henry, but both of them looked away as if nervous. Interesting.

Marco turned with a hand on my back and spoke quietly, "I understand officers, as you can see she's perfectly fine. In fact, if there is anywhere you should be worried about her going, it's back home."

"What?" One of them asked my heart sped up.

He continued keeping his gaze on me while playing with my hair, "additionally, please refrain from making up bullshit. I'm well aware her mother's boyfriend was in the parking lot after school, watching her."

Really? Oh, that is just weird.

"Do me a favor," Marco spoke quietly, ignoring their reactions, "I understand that you have to take her back, but inform your alpha that I need security placed there until Saturday. I will extend our agreement for the contractors on the West cabins until July."

Both of them nodded and Marco turned to me, bending down slightly making me smile because we were eye to eye. "You call me if there are any issues tonight, promise?"

"I promise," I whispered and impulsively leaned forward to press a kiss to his cheek. He let out a low sound before crushing me to him, I relaxed into it. I walked towards the officers and Henry's voice was sharp and hard, making my skin shiver and not in a bad way.

"Officers," Henry chimed. "It would be in your very best interest to ensure our mate stays safe. You understand, correct?"

It clicked then. The way he used it made the concept click perfectly. My eyes widened as I looked back at Marco. Animals had mates and they were shifters... did that mean they wanted to mate with me? I frowned and Atlas made a low worried noise as I walked towards the door and out into the cold rainy atmosphere. Well, talk about something to freakin' think about.

"Maya," Ledger's voice called out as he ducked out and offered me a heavy jacket that swamped me in his scent. I smiled at him and he kissed my cheek before I slid into the back of the SUV. Luckily, the police bars were on the third row so I didn't feel like I was in trouble.

"Now, Miss Maya," one of the cops, his shiny head making me smile, as he turned back. "We do apologize for having to take you home. Is there anything specific you would like to report in reference to your family?"

Three more days. Don't be dramatic now.

"No," I stated softly. "It's fine."

Both of them shared a look, but I kept quiet as my mood plummeted the closer we got to the house. I really hadn't realized how late it was when we got back from flying and as we drove up to the trailer the other cop spoke, his beard spotted with gray unlike Atlas'.

"We are going to walk you to the door, Maya. and just remember we are going to be outside all night if you need anything, Mr. Moretti is an essential part of the shifter community. We all owe him in some way or another."

I wondered if that had to do with his business.

As we stepped out of the car, my mother and Jed opened the door, glaring at me. I shivered under the jacket and before I could step closer, the officers spoke.

"Maya was over at someone's house doing homework, as she had informed you," Mr. Shiny Head stated, sounding frustrated. "Next time please refrain from calling the cops unless necessary."

Jed smiled with his gross, rotten teeth, "of course."

"Another thing," Mr. Beard stated, "we've received reports of disturbances and yelling on this block, so we are going to be outside the house all night. I just wanted to let you folks know."

Both of them went serious and I felt my smile nearly peak out. There was absolutely no hiding what the officers meant, it was clear. I turned back to them and flashed a kind smile before walking past Jed and my mother. Once inside I sped walk into my room and locked it, shoving a chair underneath it and opening my window. Just in case I needed to scream or crawl out.

It was quiet for a few minutes and I watched as the police officers parked in sight of my room. I was so glad to have friends like Marco and my other boys. Then again, I think I had realized that when they said 'mate' they didn't mean friend or buddy. So what the heck did they mean? The devil inside of me told me to keep my mouth shut. To not comment about how I didn't deserve their affection, or possible love.

Don't say anything.

The voice inside of me was vibrant and begging. I sighed sitting down on my torn mattress and drawing my knees up. When a harsh voice pressed against my door, I became even more thankful for the vigilant eyes on the house.

"They can't stay out there forever, little bitch," Jed's voice crawled against my skin as I refused to answer. I turned off my lights and put my head against the wall.

I'd always felt alone. I'd always been physically hurt by my parents, but Jed was different. Jed made me fear the possibility of what he could do. I wasn't stupid and I knew there was a learning curve here for me, but he made me want to hide away. To go back to the basement I spent most of my life in. Actually, all of my life that I could remember.

I jumped when a dark shadow passed my window, but relaxed as Atlas climbed through and flashed me a brilliant white smile. Without a second thought, I made room for him and as he laid back, I crawled forward so that my body was on top of his and my cheek against his chest. That steady heart beat had my entire body relaxing as I smiled.

I wasn't alone anymore though.

I just hoped to find a way that I could keep my new friends, despite knowing they deserved better than me.

9
LEDGER

"What do you mean you lost her?" I demanded my temper flaring, which was unusual on its own course. I was a relaxed guy. Really. Most of the time. Okay to be fair, not always.

"I mean," Anani bit out, "that it was between class periods and she went to go use the washroom and never came back out."

"Did you check the bathroom?" I raised a brow.

My brother leveled me with a look and said, "you must think I'm the dumbest motherfucker around."

Henry whistled at the end of the long hall and both of us looked over, as he nodded towards the pavilion doors. We jogged down the way and the cold air smacked into our faces as my eyes widened.

Do you ever see anything that truly shocks you?

My twin and I weren't strangers to violence, none of us were. Before we'd broken away from our families, we'd been trained in the military within the realm we came from. I was around fourteen when Marco had finally decided to move our flight out of the Dreki realm. Ever since then, we'd made the rocky transition from being a group of shifters to acting like normal high school students.

A difficult feat.

I had gotten used to my life though, the lack of violence and excitement. So when I'd seen Lorn teasing a tiny little thing with dark hair, everything inside of me had washed with anger. Very unlike me. It wasn't until her gold eyes met mine that I'd realized we were mates. A true shock to the system.

But not nearly as bad as this.

"Why aren't we interrupting this?" I hissed out.

Henry shook his head, "we can't. I'm not sure how she did it, but the entire circle around the two of them is blocked off."

I could see the golden ring of magic and I looked around to see only a few shifters outside watching in shock as Becky cornered Maya against the tree. Except Maya didn't seem upset. No, her gaze was dark and something about what Becky was saying had the opposite effect of scaring her. Our little mate was no doubt naive, but there was a strength underneath all of that golden skin and I couldn't wait until she had her feet on solid ground. I could just tell she'd be fucking unstoppable.

"What is happening?" Anani demanded.

"Becky cornered her and then Maya threw up the shield around them. She's not scared, but very defensive. I can't hear what they are saying," Henry said softly.

I stepped closer and placed my hand against the smooth almost sparkling dome shape. I assumed humans couldn't see it, but none of them approached, so maybe there was some property to this I wasn't understanding. Then again, I had no idea what she freakin' is, so maybe I'm just making shit up. Maya's eyes met mine for a moment and I went to warn her as Becky slapped her. It caused my little mate to hit her head against the back of the tree. Rage filtered through my system.

I think I expected a lot to happen.

What I didn't expect to happen? A look of fury to cross her face that was so unlike Maya, it had me actually stilling because I felt as though there was a predator in the area that even my dragon was unsure of. Maya, without pretense, stepped into her space and spoke what looked to be harsh words. Becky flinched and stepped back, but Maya simply stepped forward, her eyes darkening. When Becky turned to run, she hit right into the barrier, shattering it, and releasing a piercing, almost bird-like sound that had our little mate smiling.

Then the most unexpected thing yet happened. Becky's hair went up in flames.

Holy shit. Maya stood there watching as the human was able to douse her hair with water. She was only able to save maybe a few inches lower than her jaw. Her friends were so focused on helping her, they didn't catch the incredulous look the shifters were offering her. Maya watched nearly amused before she sighed and turned back to us, all three of us with our mouths open.

"Firefly?" I asked quietly.

She offered me a soft smile, "hey you."

"What was that?" Anani demanded.

She twisted her lips. "She threatened to cut my hair off if I didn't stay away from you, so I told her she wasn't your friend. I was. She got even more mad and we went back and forth a bit. At first, I was scared but then when she slapped me, I got this odd feeling right at the center of my chest and I got angry. I am not sure how her hair burnt off, but I'm not complaining. That's horrible of me, right?"

My smile grew more and more as she talked because it was very clear that Maya was very much a shifter. The possessive, protective, and aggressive qualities were small, but very much there. Henry stepped forward and he pressed a hand to her forehead frowning before meeting our gaze with actual shock. "I think I may know what she is."

The doors opened and our principal stepped out, a very upset Becky Ash following after. Guess we would have to wait to find out. Maya froze, the bravado from earlier slipping slightly and I realized that it may have been a bit of a size thing. Becky was close in height to Maya, but the principle was a lot larger. It made me wonder how long people larger than her had been hurting her. I wrapped a possessive arm around her center.

"Maya, is it?" The principal asked, his mustache a dirty blonde like his murky eyes.

"It is," she whispered.

"Is it true you burned off Becky's hair?"

Anani chuckled, "now how in the hell would she have done that?"

Becky got angry and snapped, "she did! After I slapped her, I stepped back..."

"You slapped her?" The principal stated as Becky flushed. "Yes, but that isn't..."

"Mr. Lark," a voice rang out, "Becky is lying, clear as day. If anyone should be concerned about their safety, it's Maya."

Henry let out a low sound as Seth approached, his eyes amused and his scent distinctly dog. Maya offered him a small smile and that made me irrationally mad. I pressed my lips to her shoulder as I resisted the urge to bite right down into her soft skin. I wouldn't do that though, not until she realized we were mates. Then you better believe I'd be marking her cute little ass.

The principal looked between all of us before pinning us with a look. "Could you meet me in my office, Ms. Ash? Now. Maya feel free to call someone to pick you up if you feel uncomfortable being here right now, just make sure to inform the school."

Becky tossed Maya a narrowed eye glance as the woman in my arms shook with tension and let out a low dangerous soft sound. I felt everything harden at it and she flicked her eyes up at me as I offered her an apologetic cocky smile.

I mean, did she actually expect my cock to not get hard with her firm little ass pressed against it in a school skirt?

Fucking shit. The way she'd casually thrown out those words the other night was something fucking magical. Seeing that soft plush mouth form the word 'cock' and talk about 'fucking' had me wanting to bend her over and teach her all about that shit.

"Marco is on his way," Henry offered as I tugged her towards the parking lot.

I could hear Henry and Anani talking quietly behind me, so I decided to distract her. "So how was last night when you got home?"

She nibbled her lip before answering, "it was good, Atlas stopped by."

"Did they say anything?" I asked directly. She could not admit it all she wanted, but I was very fucking aware of how those bruises appeared there. When you were abused as a child, you could easily recognize it in others. It was one of the reasons I was hesitant to ever raise my voice around Maya because even if it was in excitement, I could see her flinch. I wanted to get her into our house so she could become use to it and relax as soon as possible.

I knew it had been barely three days since I'd met her, but something in me had fundamentally changed. I'd follow this woman anywhere. I looked down at her as those gold, thick lashed eyes met mine and dark chocolate and gold hair shifted gently around her angled face. God. She was so fucking beautiful.

I barely looked away as Marco's BMW pulled up.

"Angel," Atlas called out as she looked at him and offered a smile. I loved that about Maya. She never held back. Never played games. Her emotions were right there and I could tell that when she didn't want to say something, she tried to find a way around lying. She had to be one of the most authentic women I'd ever met.

Her plush lips moved as she said goodbye to my brother and Henry, before moving closer to me. My arms wrapped around her as I buried my nose in her hair, absorbing her scent. I could smell the ash more prominent on her skin than ever. I think I knew Henry's theory on what she was and after what I'd seen today, I couldn't even disagree with him.

She was more unique than she'd ever realize and not just because of what she shifted into.

I watched as she got into the car and I slid my hands in my pants pocket, the other two and myself wishing that we were leaving with them. Unfortunately, if we were going to play human, then human rules applied to us. Those golden eyes looked back at us one more time before they left the parking lot and I shook my head.

Nothing was ever going to be the same now that I'd met Maya, and I was perfectly okay with that.

10

MAYA

"You burnt off her hair?" Sai grinned, his eyes glinting with something I didn't recognize.

"Only half of it, and I have no idea how I did it," I yawned slightly as Atlas turned with a worried look.

"Did you not sleep well?" He frowned.

"I did," I nodded. "It's just been a lot of new experiences these past three days."

"Well, you're about to have another," Marco noted, "we are stopping at the mall before going home."

Home. I wish it was my home.

Wasn't that the hardest part about all this? I could defend and protect my boys all I wanted, but at the end of the day, Becky was right. They weren't mine, and eventually they'd leave this area and I would be left with just driving past their massive empty mansion every so often. Oh wait! I didn't even flippin' know how to drive. I felt my lips dip slightly before I tried to hide it.

"What's wrong?" Sai asked immediately.

"Nothing," I shook my head, not wanting to really bother him with it.

I squeaked as the car came to a stop and both Marco and Atlas looked back at me as well. Cars honked around us and I raised my brows because while I didn't know much about driving, I knew this wasn't right.

"What's wrong?" Marco repeated Sai's question.

I sighed, "it really isn't worth having all these angry humans honk at you."

"Maya," Atlas demanded.

I sighed, "I was just thinking about how long the six of you were planning to stay in the area and it made me sad to realize you may leave. *There!* Come on, I don't like the honking noise."

Marco frowned, "why would we leave?"

"We wouldn't leave you, Maya," Sai pointed out.

See, that? *That* frustrated me. I shook my head and ran a hand through my hair. "Can we please go?" I watched out the window until they started moving again. I was frustrated because you couldn't just say that to someone. You couldn't just say you wouldn't leave them. They couldn't promise me that.

Before I knew it, we came to a massive mall that seemed to be made up of a cross shape of shops that all connected through open air walkways. Didn't seem very smart to me, considering the weather. I shook myself, promising I'd be in a good mood while we were here.

Marco's hand caught mine and I smiled up at him, liking how his rough palm felt against my soft one, his eyes searching my face before offering me a smile as well. Butterflies jumped in the center of my chest as I focused on the steps ahead.

"He's right, you know," he whispered softly as we entered under a terrace. "We wouldn't leave you."

I frowned, "You have to stop saying stuff like that, Marco."

He made a low noise and paused, tilting my chin up, "Absolutely not. Why would I stop?" I was glad the other two had walked ahead.

I sighed, "Marco, I'm barely friend material, let alone someone you should base your life around. If you guys have to leave town, then you have to leave."

His eyes darkened, "What do you mean you're barely friend material?"

I shrugged, "I am a bit weird. I growl. I set people's hair on fire and my mom has yet to be proven wrong about the devil thing. I'm just saying, you could do a lot better."

A low rumble came from his throat as he shook his head, "I really hope your birthday is sooner than Saturday."

I frowned, "What?"

"Then you will understand what is going on here, honey," he muttered and fixed me with a demanding gaze. "Do something for me?"

"Sure," I whispered.

"For the next few days, just enjoy this, okay? I promise you, we aren't going anywhere. In fact, I think you'll find we are going to grow a bit overbearing."

"Impossible," I mumbled as his smile softened.

Marco slipped an arm around my waist. "Come on. I have to prove to you the overbearing aspect of my personality."

I grinned. "Doubtful, but willing to give it a chance."

∼

OVERBEARING MAY NOT BE the right word.

The three of them were insane. I mean actually insane. I was buried in a pile of things I had no idea what to do with, and every time I insisted they didn't need to buy it, they did. The worst part? It was my own curiosity's fault. I liked touching and looking at things. I didn't realize it at first, but whenever I showed an interest in an item, it ended up being brought to the dressing room. Now I was standing with the clothing lady, feeling absolutely overwhelmed.

"I don't understand why they are doing this," I muttered.

"Be happy," she chuckled. "Some man spending this much money on me? I wouldn't refuse."

I frowned though. Wasn't that the point? They didn't need to do this. In fact, I preferred they didn't. I looked around knowing they were waiting and planned to tell them what I thought. I picked up a light pink jacket.

"That jacket is one of my favorites," she commented and helped me into it, closing it around my waist and then running the belt through it. "See? It has a bow in the back."

I turned my head and it did in fact, have a bow in the back. It was actually really pretty.

With a nod I stood out to the boys and all of them looked up with big smiles. I flushed and paused, "what?"

"Freakin' adorable," Sai muttered.

Marco tilted his head and grinned, "does that have a bow on the back of it?"

I nodded and turned as Atlas chuckled making a comment about something regarding a present. I remembered my mission then.

"Listen," I turned towards them, "I really like the stuff, but I can't accept all this. I won't use your money."

"We are buying it either way, so you either pick what

you want or go with whatever we pick," Marco explained softly.

Sai offered me a smirk, "to be honest, I like the sound of that."

"I'm only buying what I need," I stated softly while crossing my arms. I wasn't budging on this. Atlas whistled.

"Damn Marco," he chuckled, "she's actually serious."

Marco stood up and walked forward slowly, but with every step, my heart beat faster and faster until I realized I was backing up and the large man had me caged against the wall. He tilted his head and narrowed his eyes.

"Why?" He demanded softly.

"Because I don't want to spend your money. Friendships are supposed to be equal, and this isn't equal," I stated softly, but confidently.

Those darkening eyes searched mine as he made a low frustrated noise before muttering something about 'why the fuck do I have this money then?'

I raised a brow as he backed off and Sai offered me a cheeky smile. "Impressive, Maya."

"Oh!" I remembered, "I meant to ask, yesterday when I was leaving you said 'mate'..."

The store attendant walked out as all the men's eyes widened in warning, I turned and offered her a smile. I hoped they could answer my question later. She led me into the massive dressing room and for the next hour, had me try on an assortment of outfits. Some winter and some summer. All of them very pretty. Labels that said 'Vineyard Vines' and 'Hilfiger' passed me and when she asked what I wanted to wear out of here, I stopped confused. I looked at my uniform and she laughed.

"I heard they are taking you out to an early dinner," she whispered conspiratorially. "Want me to pick?"

"Sure," I nodded and she handed me a black A-line skirt with a bow at the waist and a purple sweater that I knew tucked into it. The edge was lace by the collar and matched the patterns of the tights she handed me. Before I changed into everything, including the leather boots she offered, she held up a finger as if forgetting something.

"I grabbed these while you were trying stuff on." She pulled out a cart and my eyes went wide. *Holy crap.* I'd never seen that many pairs of lace thongs and boyshorts in my life. Which isn't unsurprising, but there were lace items that crossed and hooked and did a bunch of other stuff I wasn't sure of. She chuckled and patted my hand.

"I'm going to pack it all up, I went with a lot of lace and pastel as well as some darker colors for the winter," she chimed, "but first try this one, its a 34C, so I imagine it will fit."

I wasn't shy about my body at all, so I easily removed my thin white bra and underwear to trade for purple lace. I slid it on my body and instantly felt like I'd transformed into one of those magazine models. True excitement filled me as I squeaked in excitement seeing myself in the mirror.

As I mentioned, I was thin, but this made me look curvy. My breasts were pushed up and the lace cut across my butt cheeks and emphasized my small waist. My dark hair was exceptionally curly today. I looked good.

"Angel?" Atlas called, "you okay?"

"I'm great," I confirmed, not realizing how damn confident I sounded.

"Oh for Christ's sake," a deep voice echoed as both of us turned and saw Atlas, who had peaked in to make sure. His eyes raked my body before turning and leaving the dressing room attendant laughing. It got even worse as Sai and Marco both looked in, confused. Sai just looked angry and

Marco had this odd, dazed expression before turning on his heel.

Oh! I bet they felt all weird and flushed like I had when I saw Ledger's abs. I understood that.

"You've got those boys wrapped around your finger," she commented, grinning. "Ah, to be young again. Come on, let's get you ready to go so I can organize for this to be delivered today."

I frowned down at my finger because I wasn't positive how to tell her they were much too big for that.

Once dressed, I tugged on the same pea coat but in black and organized my uniform in a tote bag that matched this dark purse I now owned. It was pretty neat. I walked out through the curtains to find all my men looking intently at me.

"I'm ready," I chimed.

"Oh, I'm ready as well," Sai muttered, looking like he meant something else.

Atlas offered me an amused grin and shook his head, going to talk to the woman as Marco leaned back, raising a finger to call me over. I put my bag down and walked over, feeling really freakin' good about myself, to be honest. The minute I was in arms reach, the man wrapped his arms around my waist and tugged me forward so I had a knee on either side of him, a soft sound coming from my throat that had him stilling.

Everything inside of me heated as those mint eyes darkened and I shivered, causing a predatory flash to darken his gaze even further. I lifted a hand and ran my fingers across his lips as a shudder ran through him, his forehead falling against my cashmere covered chest.

"These clothes still aren't good enough for you," he mumbled.

I pulled back and tilted his head up, "don't say that, I love these."

"I love them as well," Atlas drawled, making me blush.

"I like what's underneath them," Sai whispered as I squeaked and a warm flush of heat crawled up my back. Oh my.

"Mr. Moretti," the woman stated, "it will be delivered to you within the hour."

I turned to her and walked right up to her, pulling her into a hug. She squeaked, but I just whispered 'thank you' because I'd never had an adult woman treat me with that much kindness. I then turned and followed Marco to the door.

"You hungry?" Sai asked, intertwined our fingers.

My stomach rumbled. "That would be a yes."

The entire air was chilled and drizzle fell on my head in a relaxing pattern. I squeezed Sai's hand tighter as we walked down the paved stone pathway toward a series of restaurants. I wasn't really paying attention to what they were talking about and I froze as we approached a smaller store front.

The door was different than the others, splattered with paint and a unique glass door handle. The sign on the door was modest and read *Clara's Craft Store*. I grinned and broke away, pulling open the door as chimes sang above me making me smile. Immediately, warmth surrounded me and the yellow color of the walls made my heart pitter-patter. You know when a place just resonates with you? That's how I felt right now.

"Angel?" Atlas called out. I was distracted though, walking across the worn wooden floors. The walls were built high with different colored shelves and a ton of craft supplies from paints to shading utensils. The center was a series of different shelves and island like surfaces, with a table at the back. A woman stood at the counter, offering me a soft smile, her warm brown eyes making me happy. She had gray hair that was covered in paint and she was wearing these jean overalls that I was jealous of.

"Hi," I chirped approaching, "what is this place?"

She laughed her voice soft and light, "this is my craft store, pretty neat, huh?"

I nodded enthusiastically, "very. I want to spend all of my time here."

That was very honest.

"Do you paint or draw?" She asked curiously and I shook my head.

"Never tried," I mentioned, "what would I start with?"

"Sweetheart," Marco's voice had me jumping as I looked up. He searched my face and I frowned.

"What?" I raised a brow.

"Nothing," Atlas patted Marco's shoulder. "We will be over there if you need us."

Sai winked, "have fun, Kitten."

Kitten? Now why did that make me blush?

"Come on," Clara, I assumed, walked me towards a large shelf in the back. She spoke quietly and with a soothing teaching voice. "What sounds more interesting to you? Painting or drawing?"

I looked over all of the different sample projects on display, and smiled, "painting."

She nodded and began to gather some supplies, "let's start you on watercolor."

I frowned noticing the pile. I really didn't want them buying me anything else. I looked up. "Is it possible for me to work here to pay off the supplies?"

Her eyes softened as she looked over my shoulder,

setting the material down. "What's your name?"

"Maya," I offered my hand as she met it introducing herself as Clara.

She sighed, "you remind me a lot of me. My Alec never wanted me buying or working for stuff, I'm assuming you are facing something similar?"

Who was her Alec?

I nodded, "I just don't like them spending money on me."

"Kitten," Sai called and I refused to look, knowing they could hear me somehow.

"How about this," she smiled, "you let them buy this stuff because I don't think they are going to give you a choice, and I give you a job here? You can work out what works best with your schedule for after school."

"How do you know I'm in school?" I frowned.

"I have a granddaughter about your age," she explained and squeezed my shoulder.

I nodded and met her hand, "deal."

As we walked back, Marco pinned me with a look and I wrapped my arms around his center, burying my face against his button down. His lips finding my ear as the other two checked out.

"You really want to work?"

"Yes," I responded softly, "I've had my entire life controlled, it feels good to make this choice."

Marco let out a low sound, "Honey, what happened before you came here?"

I froze and swallowed, "Why does it matter, Marco?"

He tightened his arms around me and spoke quietly, "Because you're our mate and I want to know everything there is about you."

There was something more to this... and I'm sorry,

what? My question from yesterday came flying back.

My head snapped up, "Mate? We aren't talking about friends, are we?"

His chest rumbled as he grasped my chin gently, searching my face. "I think you know that we aren't talking about being friends, Maya."

I winced and shook my head, "Marco…"

He pressed a kiss to the corner of my lips and I shivered, leaning closer to him. Grasping his arms as he let out a soft dangerous sound, nuzzling my neck gently. I whimpered as I felt his grip tighten.

"Marco," Sai stated carefully as Marco looked up, narrowing his eyes, but shaking his head muttering a curse. I clung onto him still.

Clara handed Atlas a bag. "How do you feel about starting this Sunday?"

I snapped out of the odd haze I was in and nodded, "I'd love that. I will be here, what time?"

"We open at noon, wear something you don't mind getting paint on."

With that, we were out the door and I tried to take the bag from Atlas, but he just tucked me under his arm. When we reached a velvet overhang, the sound of soft music in a language I didn't completely recognize came over head. It sounded a bit like French, but I only knew that because I'd listened through the floorboards to hear the old french films my mother liked.

I made the mistake of voicing this and all three men stilled as we made it through the door. I acted like what I'd said was perfectly fine and instead focused on the young man standing at the booth in the front. A million different senses hit me and a warm flush had me taking off my jacket and laying it across my arm.

"Hi there." The younger man flashed me a grin, "what can I do for you?"

"We want to eat here," I offered a smile as he chuckled like I was joking. His eyes flickered over my shoulder, "the four of you?"

I noticed all three men seemed to be having some conversation so I ignored them. I shrugged, "sure."

His grin grew as he grabbed menus, "quite the handsome entourage you have there."

My lips pressed together, "they are pretty handsome," I murmured following him. I heard footsteps behind me as Atlas' arm wrapped around me protectively. If Sai was all fire, Atlas was calm and steady, making me feel protected. Marco though made me feel like a flame was bursting out from under my skin, dangerous and extreme. At the same time, there was a contrast of safety and control he exuded.

"Calm down," the man 'tsked' to Marco's frustrated expression, "her and I bat for the same team. If anything, it's you who should be worried."

Now, I *did* know what that meant.

Father had hated men who liked other men. I didn't understand why it mattered, so I let loose a small laugh because the host seemed to find it so funny. I wiggled from Atlas and walked next to the man as he began to talk about a bunch of different foods before finally reaching the small circular booth that was lit up by candles. He winked and I slid in running my hands over the soft material of the seat as Atlas slid in on one side and Marco on the other, my eyes tracing Sai's still darkened expression.

"What can I start you with to drink?" He asked curiously.

Marco barked off some order and the man rolled his eyes, amused before walking away. I looked over the carefully polished silverware and very clear glasses. I touched my finger against the flower arrangement and realized they were very much real.

"Maya," Atlas started, "what do you mean, you used to listen to them through the floorboards?"

I frowned, confused, "I'm not sure how many different ways that can be taken."

Sai chuckled, "She makes a fair point."

Marco grunted, "Honey, I think it would help all of us if you gave us just a bit more knowledge about where you lived before this. I mean, you can't blame us, you aren't even registered with the state, Maya."

I sighed and crossed my arms, "I told you I lived in Louisiana. I lived in a church. I don't know why we need to talk more about it than that. I mean, realistically, it's over and as of this Saturday, when I turn 18, it really won't matter. Isn't that enough?"

"No," Marco stated evenly. "Can you at least tell us where the bruises were from?"

"An accident," I mumbled.

"Maya," Marco was practically begging.

"Remember earlier when you told me I should just relax and enjoy this? Well, let's do that. I can explain tomorrow if you want me to," I whispered, knowing once they realized what a freak I was, they wouldn't want to spend time with me anymore.

"Tomorrow," Atlas stated softly and I nodded.

I let out a happy hum as the waiter appeared and offered us menus. I took a moment to breathe in their different warm and fresh scents, knowing that when tomorrow came, I would at least have a job to look forward to on Sunday.

11

ANANI

*H*onestly, after the day at school we had, I expected a lot.

Maya in my house making cookies in an oversized hoodie and paint splattered face was not one of them, but I loved it. Her dark hair was in a messy bun and pale blue paint on her face as she helped Ledger make cookies. I'd literally been maybe thirty minutes behind them, how the hell did this happen?

"Peanut?" I asked as she turned to look at me with a big smile.

"Anani," she chirped, "I missed you today."

I felt my ears pinken as Henry chuckled, kissing her head in passing. Wasn't it crazy how at home this already felt? She was here and looked domestic as fuck, wandering around the kitchen and tossing out beautiful smiles. Upstairs I could hear Marco and Sai talking with the contractors who were working on her room.

"What's with the paint?" I asked curiously as her eyes warmed.

"I got a job today!" She chirped as Atlas let out a frustrated sound from the other room.

Henry rose a brow, "Where at?"

"Clara's Crafts," she chirped and rolled a cookie in her small elegant hands.

Interesting. I smiled slightly, "are you interested in crafts?"

"Can you put in the cookies?" She asked my brother sweetly.

He nodded, like the obsessed fool we all were and she dusted off her hand on the dish towel before she grabbed my hand. I followed her to the family room and instantly smiled at the large easel that stood over a plastic sheet. We rounded the corner and my eyebrows went up.

Well, fuck me.

"Have you shown this to anyone else?" I asked quietly. There was no way she had.

Maya tilted her head, "No, it's not really finished."

Not finished? It was fucking perfect. I wasn't even a fan of watercolor and this was a stunning sunset pallet that featured what seemed to be a bird pushing through the clouds on a vertical path. This couldn't be a fucking coincidence.

"Henry!" I called out.

"It's not good enough," she whispered as I shook my head.

"It's stunning Maya," I amended. Her cheeks pinkened.

Henry rounded it while adjusting his glasses. As a dragon, he shouldn't have needed glasses in all technicality. However, he had suffered from an injury early on in life that had hurt his vision, so if he wasn't shifted, it helped to wear them.

"Oh wow," he muttered, "you painted this today, Sweetheart?"

Maya nodded and twirled a brush, "Pretty neat, huh?"

Understatement of the fucking century.

"Maya!" Marco called from the stairs as she perked up. I offered Henry a look and followed her as a group of work men passed through the front door.

"Why are they here?" She asked softly, almost worried. I realized it probably looked like we were moving to her considering the exchange of furniture going on.

"Go check it out," I nodded as she jogged up the steps and one of the workers looked back at her pert ass. Motherfucker. I threw my arm out to stop his path as she rounded the corner upstairs and then I looked at the man, his face paling.

Dumb fucking humans.

"If you want to keep your job," I hissed out, "I suggest keeping your eyes where they fucking belong, understood?"

The guy nodded as his boss offered him a dirty look. Then I released my hand and let them go, muttering a curse under my breath. It wasn't very often that the darkness boiling underneath my skin came out, but with Maya, it felt like a needed quality. A necessity to protect her.

Somehow this felt like the calm before the storm.

We had seven bedrooms, well now we did as the secondary office had been turned into a bedroom for Maya. I walked down the hall and found her standing in the doorway, her eyes wide and face expressionless. I didn't blame her for having to process it. There was a lot going on. Not only did we have a stunning window panel that circled the outside of the house, but her bed was massive and I didn't think for a minute that was unintentional. All of her clothes from earlier were in the closet and her extra art supplies set up in the corner near the forest view. A soft carpet padded her feet as she walked in.

Instead of asking why, because I'm pretty sure she was starting to figure it out, she just looked around the room. It was hard, because I think instinctual parts of this were fitting together for her, but the hardest part was going to be convincing her that she was something other than human.

Then I realized she was crying.

Marco had her in his arms as I frowned approaching, her crying muffled against his shirt as I ran my hands through her hair. "Maya, Peanut , what's wrong?"

"It's so beautiful." She sniffled before muttering other words that neither of us could fully understand. I pressed my head against her shoulder and prayed for her birthday to come faster than these next two days. I needed her here. In our house. Safe and protected.

12

MAYA

I had a feeling that going home that night, things would be different tomorrow. My life was never good for long. I had a group of loving friends and they had created an entire space for me that was so beautiful, it actually made me sad. Sad because I wasn't positive how to pay them back for it. Pay them back for the real gift they'd given to me. Their friendship.

Marco drove me home that night and after some cops drove past, taking note of the property, he was given word that neither of them were home. I shivered in my crappy jacket from before, after I'd insisted that I couldn't bring any of my nice things home. My mother would destroy them. I paused at the trailer door and looked down the steps at the handsome man.

"Marco," I whispered, looking over his stunning face and expensive suit, "I don't want you coming in."

Instead of being offended, he stepped closer to me, lifting me up with an arm around the waist, and opening the door. I cringed at the low rumble that left his throat. God, it was so much worse looking at it from his point of view.

He looked around and sniffed, his eyes searching the kitchen. I closed the door and leaned against it, not sure how this would pan out. I was realizing my dragon friend was a bit intense.

"Why does it smell like your blood in here?" He bit out looking back at me.

"I'm sure I've cut myself while cooking," I murmured.

His jaw clenched as he exhaled muttering a curse and running a hand through his hair. "Maya."

"Want to see my room?" I asked as he nodded and I led him towards it. I opened it up and he ducked under the doorway, his chest letting out a more dangerous sound than before. Alright, clearly I was not going to make this man happy.

"You've been living like this all week?" He snarled.

I blushed and cringed slightly, "It's not that bad."

Marco was pissed though, "Not bad, Maya? I don't even want to consider what you deem as bad then."

I flinched back slightly and a small growl came from my throat, "You're being mean, Marco."

The man's eyes widened slightly as he then looked away muttering in a different language under his breath. I watched carefully as he closed the bedroom door, slipping the chair under the knob and kicking off his shoes.

"What are you doing?" I asked quietly.

He raised a brow before answering, "Atlas has a job tonight and I don't want you sleeping alone."

"You don't have to," I whispered, not wanting to be a burden.

"I know," he stated softly beckoning me down to the bed, "but I want to."

I curled on my side, facing him as his eyes darkened on my expression and he wrapped his arms and hooked a leg over mine. A peace took over me. I fell asleep so easily and that should have been the first sign something was wrong.

When I woke, I wasn't positive I was awake at first. But why would Jed be in my dreams? I froze as the man offered me a snear and took the safety off the gun he pointed at Marco's sleeping form. I had no idea how he hadn't woken up yet, but then I realized the door had never been opened. How the heck did he fit in through the window?

"Shhh," Jed spoke quietly, "I want to make something very clear, little bitch."

Why did this not feel right?

Everything was hazy and lethargic, like I was moving through space and time at a slower rate. I wanted to shake Marco awake but it was like he was knocked out. My pulse picked up and I began to tremble authentically.

"Jed," I whispered.

He moved the gun closer to his head and leaned forward. "If I find them here again, in any capacity, I'll kill them."

Something fierce inside of me threatened to break out, but when his hand closed around my throat, I started to choke. That was when things got even more odd. Because I could feel someone shaking me and whispering me name, but I was also losing consciousness.

He was going to kill Marco.

"Marco," I sobbed as Jed let go of my throat and the air around me turned crisp, everything snapping into reality. A soothing voice was talking to me, but I was afraid to open my eyes. Afraid to see that Marco was dead.

He couldn't be.

"Honey," he whispered gently, "I'm right here, Maya. I need you to open your eyes. Please."

"He tried to kill you," I lamented in a gasp as I sobbed

into Marco's shirt and he soothed my hair. I knew rationally he wasn't dead. I wasn't stupid. Yet, even his vanilla pine scent couldn't completely calm me down. I needed more. I needed to open my damn eyes. They stung slightly as I did but a pair of clear mint green eyes met mine in a commanding soft way.

"I'm right here," he whispered, "who tried to kill me, Maya?"

"Jed," I shivered and placed my head down feeling nearly sick to my stomach.

Right then, a pounding on my door had me pressing further into him. "Little bitch, you better be asleep. I don't want to hear any of your fucking crying."

He was drunk and I covered the rumble that came from Marco's mouth as I tried to be as quiet as possible. I shivered against his frame as the wind from outside the wind cascaded against my heated, tear filled face.

"Maya!" He pounded on the door again, "answer me, you fucking bitch."

Hadn't he just said I better be asleep?

"Jed!" My mother's raspy voice called out, "come here Baby."

I was trembling and shaking, my skin ice cold as his footsteps led away. I looked at Marco and the fury in his gaze had me panicked. He spoke softly and determined, "You are done living here."

He didn't even know the half of it. I nodded and put my head against his large chest, relaxing into the man I'd grown to trust so much. His dragon made a soft compelling noise that had me relaxing as I closed my eyes.

I was so thankful the gun had been a dream.

A larger reality hit me in the chest though, the reason I hadn't wanted to get close. I didn't want them getting hurt.

Didn't want them put in the line of fire. My shoulder blades hurt like they wanted to move and my body was flushed with heat. I could feel a change coming, but I had no fucking idea what it was.

My eyes fluttered shut on the thought that I probably needed to find a way to distance myself from the boys. Something that felt damn near impossible.

I WAS STARTING to understand the complaints others offered about school. My mind was a foggy mess since the night before and as I sat in my afternoon classes, post lunch, I began to let my mind wander. I began to consider the implications of my birthday on Saturday.

I knew that the boys wanted me to stay. But I wasn't naive enough to think they'd be around forever. Eventually I would need to fend for myself. I was glad I had that job because I could at least create a small savings, not that I knew how to open a bank account or if I even could considering my lack of a Social Security number, something I found to be rather important.

The boys sat behind me and when I turned to the twins, both of them looked up, Henry was taking enough notes, no doubt for the both of us. I searched their faces and smiled, noticing their lack of a textbook. "You didn't really have this class with me, did you?"

Anani flashed a smile, "We do now."

"Why?" I whispered softly.

Ledger tossed out the damn phrase everyone had been using, "Because you're our mate."

Tonight I was going to get some damn answers about what that entailed in the long run. If it meant what I thought it did, I was worried. When the bell rang, I stood up and walked to the front, dropping off the in class assignment we'd done and offering my teacher a smile.

"How are you adjusting Maya?" She asked, her voice soft and understanding. Ms. Gabriel was actually one of the more understanding and friendly teachers.

"Okay," I smiled, "better than I expected."

Wasn't that the truth.

"You ready?" Henry asked as I wished her goodbye and stepped into the hallway. The air was chilled and I could feel eyes on me, making me feel self conscious despite being dressed perfectly fine. Better than fine, my pleated skirt was fresh and my shoes shiny. I looked flippin' great.

People stared and talked as we walked by, Henry frowning as a chill of dread crawled up my spine. I froze as I saw Becky Ash standing ahead surrounded by a bunch of photographs on the floor and a massive poster like collage on what I could assume was my locker from the distance.

Why did I feel like this day was about to get far worse?

"Henry," Anani stated, "we need to get her..."

"Oh Maya!" Becky called as my back straightened and I shook off the twins trying to pull me. I swallowed down and crossed my arms in a defensive posture.

"What, Becky?" I asked, feeling colder than usual.

"I just wanted to repay the favor of you burning off my hair." She flashed a dirty smirk before tossing a series of extra photos on the ground, "wouldn't want your new boyfriends to be unaware of what trailer trash you were after all."

Oh no.

I kept my face blank as laughter exploded around me and someone tugged on my sleeve. I knelt down and picked up the photos covering the hallway. My mother sitting on the porch smoking a cigarette in her nightgown. My small body curled up on a threadbare mattress through the window. My torn, bloody, hoodie in the trash along with a million other beer cans and shit, that I prayed would distract away from it. Every evidence of my pathetic life was here and man, did it look rough. I looked horrible. I looked... like trash.

I swallowed down any violent tendencies and stood up to address Becky. She was closer than I expected. "Don't forget the fact your mom beats you because even she doesn't fucking want you."

My eyes flickered over to the locker where a picture of my mom holding my hair in the kitchen window and yelling at me was blown up. I cringed but still couldn't figure out what to say next. Henry was talking in harsh tones but I was just feeling a sense of humiliation. And fury. Who did this to someone?

Meeting Becky's gaze, I examined the manic look in her eyes and cruel sneer on her face. This meant a lot to her. What did it mean to me? Nothing. Really though, I was never going to see these people again after I graduated.

"I'm not sure what you were trying to accomplish?" I spoke, my voice steady as everyone stilled around me.

"To fucking expose you for the fraud you are, no amount of nice clothing or shopping is going to make up for the trash that you reek of."

"How do you know we went shopping?" I asked quietly.

Her face turned pink, "I wanted to expose all of this bullshit, followed you to see what other shady shit you were doing."

I see.

Something inside of me clicked and I stepped forward towards her and over the pictures. "Becky, I understand what you were attempting to accomplish, but as I would assume how most of your endeavors pan out, it was unsuccessful. Completely. You care about this much more than I do and it would be smart of you to not confuse my kindness for being a doormat. What I would suggest is that you clean this up, I never stated I was anything more than those pictures suggest. All it is evidence of, is that you followed me around enough to capture it on film."

Becky's mouth popped open as I pressed a finger underneath it, closing it effectively. I turned on my heel as a shriek echoed in my ears and I was yanked back, hard. I hissed as my head snapped back on the hard floor as everything went to hell around me. Her shoe hit my rib as the yelling grew louder and my body was snatched up by Henry, a few people restraining the manic woman who'd clearly lost her mind.

I swallowed, meeting her gaze as she practically foamed at the mouth like a rabid animal, I clutched onto Henry as the cool air hit my skin and I relaxed into it. The police arrived and Anani spoke to the man I'd met before, my eyes stinging and my ears ringing.

Once we were in the car, my ears popped and I relaxed into the seat the sound of my heart beat loud and wild. I realized then that Anani was yelling.

"Fucking mental ward is where she belongs," he spit out, "Who attacks someone like that?!"

I placed a hand on his leg as he startled and then Ledger muttered out, "A crazy bitch."

Alright, I almost laughed at that.

"Sweetie," Henry spoke quietly, "we are stopping at the local branch to talk to Marco, is that okay? Or do you need the hospital?"

I lifted a hand to the back of my head and pulled away,

making the twins growl at the blood there. "No, it's fine," I mumbled, "it means it will heal."

"That's fucked up," Ledger groaned.

I ignored him as we pulled into a low gray building that had a familiar BMW parked out front. I could already feel the wound on the back of my head healing as I inhaled the fresh air. Immediately, without waiting for the others, I was through the door and searching for Marco.

"Can I help you?" A stunning woman at the front door asked. I scowled at her narrowed gaze at me.

"Doubtful," I muttered and spoke louder, "where is Marco?"

"In a meeting," she responded right away and I watched her cringe as Marco rounded the corner.

"Cecile," Marco stated, his tone harsh, "If you ever turn her away from this office, you're going to find yourself without a job."

I tried not to stick my tongue out at her because I'm an adult. Although I had a day and a half...

Cecile's eyes widened, "You didn't tell me that you'd found..."

"Well I have," Marco stated, "she has the same privileges as any of my brothers, understood?"

"Yes, sir," she muttered. I walked over to Marco and he tilted his head looking alarmed.

"Why are you bleeding?" He asked turning me and lifting my hair up as I hissed. The other men entered into the office and Henry was explaining before Marco could bark out orders.

I, in the meantime, could only appreciate how modern and beautiful the office was. I really needed to know more about what my friend did. A voice inside of me argued with the label. *Mate.* I still had no idea what that meant, but a small part of me had hoped that it meant this was something bigger than just our friendship. The other part of me knew I wasn't worthy of that.

"Get Johnson on the phone," Marco bit out, "I want her institutionalized or something, we need to slap a restraining order on this immediately."

Cecile, I had to admit, moved fast, and that alone was impressive. I watched as she opened up a phone line and Anani took it from her, his words fluent and in a different language. I was a bit jealous to be honest. I wanted to speak more languages.

"It's healing," Marco noted more quietly.

"It's because it broke skin," I noted, just as quiet.

He searched my expression as a dark light filtered through his gaze. I knew my time for secrets was over. That was okay. One could only bear that weight for so long. I listened as he arranged to leave the office and I mentally prepared myself to lose the only people I'd ever cared about like this. I wrapped my jacket around me tighter as we walked out of the office, Cecile quickly looked down when I caught her staring at me. The other boys went towards the car we'd arrived in, but Marco led me towards his BMW.

Once he had made sure I was buckled in, the handsome man rounded the car that had already been started and was fairly warm.

Marco spoke quietly looking at me, "She's wrong, you know that right?"

"Wrong?" I frowned.

He grasped my hands and kissed the tops of them softly, "You are the furthest thing from trash, Maya. You are fucking perfect. Don't let her words affect you for even a moment."

I hadn't even been thinking of her comments. *Why?*

Because I knew that he wouldn't think I was perfect for long. My secrets had reached their expiration date. I sighed taking just a moment to appreciate how good he smelled. How peaceful the car was, because I just knew.

 I knew the moment that I started talking and told them everything, things would be different. So when Marco grabbed my hand, I squeezed it. What else was there to do?

13

MAYA

I stepped into their house and wrapped my arms around myself, suddenly feeling as though everyone was asking for the same god damn thing from me. I decided to take a moment and went up the stairs towards my bedroom and no one followed. Not *my* bedroom. The bedroom they put my stuff in. I removed my school shoes and went to go put on a pair of leggings and a hoodie with slippers. What? I was a bit of a pleasure seeker. I didn't bother unpacking my backpack, instead I brought it back downstairs, leaving it by the door.

Marco was already sitting in the formal living space and Atlas was leaning over a laptop with Anani. Sai was watching me and there was almost a nervous vulnerability to it while Ledger handed me a cup of tea. I really didn't want one. Henry patted the seat next to him and I sat down crossing my legs in front of themselves before breathing in.

"Her father is claiming she was off her medication," Atlas states, "she's going to get the help she needs, but I am filing a restraining order."

Oh yeah. *Becky*. I lifted a hand to the back of my head

and could feel the dry flakes of blood on my scalp. I had to give her this, she knew how to do some damage I suppose. My mom would like her.

A nervous prickle went over my skin, but it didn't feel like it had just to do with this damn situation. No, instead, it felt larger than that. Felt like a flush was overruling my skin and my center was heating up from my ribcage out. I tightened my hands on my legs as I tried to breathe through it because now was not the time to not feel well.

"Maya," Marco opened his mouth, and instantly I was talking.

"I really don't know what you want me to say Marco," I whispered immediately. I didn't.

He stilled as everyone watched my expression, tears filling my eyes.

"Maybe this isn't a good idea," Henry stated softly.

"We need to know," Marco stated as frustration built in my chest.

"Why?" I asked for the millionth time.

"Because we are your god damn mates and you come into our town bruised and fucking battered. We need some answers Maya," Sai snapped out, causing me to growl with frustration.

"You still haven't even explained what this mate thing is!" I exclaimed sitting forward. "And don't bullshit me about being just friends, because that's a lie."

The room went quiet as Sai rose a brow. "You swore."

"Yes I did," I blushed. Sai's eyes infused with a bit of amusement before flashing dark again.

"We need to explain," Ledger stated his body next to mine as he intertwined his hand with my own. I fought the urge to pull away because my frustration was misplaced, I was angry that I had to tell them the truth.

I watched as Atlas closed the laptop and Anani spoke, "Who wants to explain?"

"Oh my god," I groaned, "someone please explain."

Henry snickered and then Marco began talking.

"Alright Maya." He sat forward and I tried to give my best attention. "We are shifters, dragon shifters, and you are most definitely some type of shifter. One that we've narrowed down to two possibilities, but we can talk about that later. The point is, shifters have mates. Mates are your fated partner, or partners, that the part of your soul connected to your animal matches. Once you find them, you stay with them for the rest of your life."

I swallowed nervously, "That makes sense."

"Yeah, that was the easier part," Sai muttered.

Marco frowned slightly. "Maya, you're our mate. You would have realized it yourself on your eighteenth birthday when it fully sets in, but leaving you in the dark, I understand, is unfair."

The first thing that hit me was the spark of joy in the center of my chest. Because holy crap. They really weren't just my friends. Then that was run over by two bulldozers. One of them being the concept that this was fated. So in a way, it was an obligation. They don't have a choice in how they feel. Secondly, they deserved better and fate was cruel. Fate was cruel for putting someone so damaged with them so perfect.

"All six of you?" I whispered.

Henry nodded cautiously as I nibbled my lip. "And you said this was fated? As in, there really wasn't a choice on how you would feel about me?"

Everyone seemed to still at that as Atlas spoke, "It's not like that Maya."

"But it sort of is," I whispered.

"Maya," Marco started.

I shook my head and stood up walking to distance myself just a little bit. This was good. Which was why I wanted to cry right? *Good one, Maya.* No. This was okay. I just needed to tell them what was happening. Just needed to explain what a freak I was because they deserve so much better.

"I was locked inside a church basement from as early as I can remember," I stated my voice sounded distant. Enough so that I didn't really feel the serious shift in the room, my eyes trained on the forest greenery outside.

"My mother has never directly stated that I was adopted, but as I got older it became more clear that I wasn't her or Pastor Malcolm's biological child. She said they tried to baptize me, but that I set myself on fire because the devil didn't want my soul cleansed. From that day forward, I was locked in the basement year round. My father, Pastor Malcolm, would come down each day and read scripture to me and provide me with school material. He said that one day I would help their religious organization move forward and possibly make more just like me. Once he died, my mother took me from there and she began calling it a cult, so I began to realize that my situation growing up was far from normal. Before that, I would have assumed the beatings were normal. She said that the reason I healed was because of the devil, because the devil fixed me. Whenever any blood would spill I would heal, so she began to bruise me instead. I don't know why she keeps me around if she hates me enough to always want to hurt me."

I inhaled and continued, "I'm a freak." My voice sounded strangled. "I'm never going to be normal. I will always be playing catch up to where I should be in life. I can't even say my mother was wrong because I do have the devil inside of me. Why else would I keep being friends with all of you when I know that I shouldn't? When I know I'm not even good enough to have friends like you?"

I sniffed and wrapped my arms around myself, "I turn 18, this Saturday, and when I do, I'm gone. My mom doesn't care where I go, or what happens to me. And I know you mentioned me staying with all of you, but I don't think that's a good idea. I'm sure you understand now that... Henry!"

My back hit the wall as a pair of furious silver eyes peered down at me, the oxygen leaving the room as I shivered against his body heat. I had never felt more cold in my life. Especially because the man in front of me was vibrating with heat. Remember the other part of Henry I had mentioned sensing? It was very much out to play.

"I need you to listen to me, Maya," he whispered softly, his voice sounded dangerous.

Tears welled in my eyes knowing that he was going to tell me to leave. I was shaking so hard that he had to hold my shoulders to stop the impending panic attack.

"You. Are. Not. Leaving," he whispered softly, almost with venom at the idea.

What?

"What?" I echoed tears leaking down my face.

"I said you are not leaving. You aren't leaving tonight and you sure as hell aren't going back to your mother. I understand, Sweetheart,." he inhaled, a furious light in his eyes, "I understand that your mother has convinced you of some really fucked up shit."

Oh, he swore.

"You are not leaving though. I won't let you. You aren't a freak and you deserve a hell of a lot more than we can probably ever give you. But you are not leaving. You belong here and if you want to be our friend..."

"Mate," I voiced quietly as warmth filled his gaze.

"If you are okay with being with us," he whispered, "then we want nothing more than for you to stay."

I examined his face and voiced my last concern, "but what about the fated..."

"I don't think that matters," Henry stated softly, "I think if I was a human, I'd feel this way about you, Maya. You're absolutely perfect."

Perfect?

A small pained sound came from my throat and I buried my head in his chest. He soothed me as I felt a body pressing in behind me and Marco's voice spoke softly, "Say you'll stay Maya."

So bossy.

"I'll stay," I whispered in a tortured quiet voice between raspy quiet tears.

I felt my knees break in relief and Henry never let go of me. I could hear the other men talking but I was losing my ability to think rationally, feeling so damn relieved that they wanted me. They wanted me to stay. With them.

"They are going to send for the police again," Anani whispered as I looked up and found his gaze red and slightly glassy. I slithered out from between Marco and Henry, wrapping my arms around him, his nose buried in my hair.

"Screw Jed," I muttered, "he's a creep."

"A creep?" Sai asked quietly.

I nodded, because at this point I might as well get it all out. "He is always trying to touch me and rub on me." I cringed at that last part, but I had no other fucking word for it. The room might as well have turned into a tundra.

Atlas's voice was sharp, "Who hurt you the night I came to visit you?"

"My mom," I whispered "because she saw me with you guys, but then the next morning, he left the bruises on my neck."

"Fucking shit," Anani muttered.

"Why didn't you say anything?" Ledger asked roughly.

"I've known you all for four days. I may be naive, but sharing my abusive mother problems off the bat seemed like a bad idea," I muttered.

"I want him taken care of," Marco spoke softly, his body frozen with this dark tension.

"Not tonight!" I whipped my head back to look at him, "please not tonight, I don't want to escalate anything until I can legally leave the house. Please, please, Marco. If I get sent back there, it is only going to be worse if we do something."

He inhaled and searched my face before nodding. I rested my cheek against Anani's chest as my dry and sore eyes sighed relief. A very small part of me was thrilled to be going to bed in the large, truly, massive bed upstairs.

I WOKE up to a room bathed in darkness and I panicked for a moment, only to have a true sigh of relief leave me. My head was surrounded by the softest pillows and the blanket over me sheltered my freshly washed skin. I had stood in the shower for at least an hour before even washing my hair. I'd used this rosemary mint shampoo and then proceeded to shave, like everywhere. That sounds weird, but my mom had no reason to teach me how to shave, so before school started I'd done a botched job of it after seeing all the women in Cosmo. This time around everything was far smoother. Even down there. That's right, Vogue called that 'trimming the lady bush' which I had to admit, made me laugh so hard I nearly cried. Who the heck came up with these titles? Maybe I needed to work for Vogue.

My body was cocooned in warmth and I was glad I'd asked the twins to stay. I wasn't sure why, but something about what I'd gone through had really messed with them. Both were shirtless and laying facing me, their dark lashes brushing against their stark skin. I could see their tattoos now and Holy Christ, were there a lot of them. I wanted to touch them but I worried I would never stop, which was a problem because I was really thirsty.

I unwrapped myself and crawled towards the end of the bed, letting my toes press against the floor. Before leaving the room, I walked towards the massive panel of windows and looked over the thick forest area highlighted by moonlight. I was surprised my mother and Jed had yet to say something or show up with the cops. My mother didn't really surprise me actually.

My feet barely made a noise as I walked downstairs and I was surprised to find, a figure in the living room. Was he having issues sleeping?

"Sai?" I asked softly as I tiptoed into the living room. I knew it was his dark head tilted down and a bottle of something sat in front of him.

I tried again, "Sai? Why aren't you in bed?"

He groaned in a pained voice and looked up, his dark eyed red rimmed and jaw tense. I froze because he seemed angry and I couldn't gauge at what.

"Maya," he said softly. "You should go to bed."

A shiver went through me as I stepped across the flooring into a plush rug, my arms wrapping around my center. I was glad I had put a robe on over my large shirt now.

"Are you okay?" I ignored him and approached carefully.

"No," he admitted, "I had no idea you'd been living like that..."

"Sai," I whispered, approaching him and looking down worried. "How could you have known? It doesn't matter anymore, anyway, I'm here and I'm okay." I felt the need to reassure this man, to make him understand that everything was okay.

He braced his arms on his knees and looked up at me, starting at my toes and up to where my hair laid in a messy bun. He grunted, "Fuck."

"What?" I asked, authentically concerned as I sat next to him, except he lifted me instantly to sit on his lap. He nuzzled my neck and took a deep breath, I looked down at him and grasped his face. I turned and found myself far closer than before, my chest meeting his. I felt my legs clench at how hard he was underneath me.

"This is dangerous," he whispered softly, almost to himself. "You aren't ready for any of this."

I wasn't 100% positive what he was talking about, but my guess was his physical form of hitting on me? I mean, his erection was pretty freakin' apparent and a small shiver of something began to crawl through me. I could still imagine how freakin' big he was and I'm sorry, but that was just interesting to me. I was curious.

"You don't know that," I spoke slowly as he met my eyes in disbelief.

"Maya," he mumbled.

I cupped his jaw and spoke softly, "I don't know a lot, Sai, and I'm not ashamed about it. I know I like you though and I just thought..."

I paused and realized what I wanted from him.

"What?" He asked softly.

I smiled softly, "Will you be my first kiss?"

I mean they said we are mates, right? I'm assuming mates will want to *mate* eventually? Like how animals do? So I should probably get that kissing part thing down. I was really interested in getting to that other part, but this was a good start, right?

An indecipherable look crossed his face as his eyes melted to a warm pool of midnight water. I waited for his answer and he hesitated for a moment, looking over my face and then my lips. I had no idea what I was doing.

"Are you sure?" His voice was husky.

I nodded, "Please."

"Christ," he mumbled before pulling me closer to him so we were nose to nose.

"I don't know how..."

But then I did. His lips met mine and a content sound came from my throat at how right this closeness felt. Going with instinct, I leaned in closer and he deepened the kiss, his hands grabbing my waist in a solid hold. I was very glad I had asked for what I wanted.

My first kiss was amazing. I didn't have a comparison chart, but I could feel my entire body growing warm as that burning ember sensation grew and my body urged me closer. I wanted to taste more of him and my tongue swept across his lips as he let out a low rumble. I found myself tangling my hands inside his hair until he finally pulled away, his cheeks flushed and eyes dark.

"Shit Maya," he whispered.

I blushed, "That was amazing, I mean, at least for me..."

He kissed me again for my answer and this kiss had a slightly different feel. I could almost feel the tension under his skin and I was shaking from the excitement in my own body. My body was keyed up for something and I had no idea what. It was like someone had filled my veins with gasoline and set fire to it.

"Sai," a warning voice called from the kitchen. I blushed and looked up, unashamed, to see Marco leaning against the doorframe. Sai groaned and put his head against my neck, I brushed his hair gently.

"Maya, beautiful, I'm going to go to bed, I don't trust myself right now," he whispered, his eyes dark.

Trust himself? Well, I trusted him. If he thought that was best...

I kissed his lips in a barely there movement. "Thanks for my first kiss."

He pulled me closer before placing me down on the couch and striding away. I could totally see how much he liked me from here. My lips curled into a smile and that was how Marco captured me.

"Hi," I whispered as he lifted me up and I wrapped my legs around his waist. I could still feel the weird energy under my skin and Marco groaned in response to it.

"I feel..." I mumbled, not knowing how to describe it. It was an odd feeling, like heat was trying to burst from my stomach but at the same time, my core was tightening with need.

He placed me on the kitchen counter and looked at me. He spoke softly, "how do you feel?"

I bit my lip not knowing how to describe it, his hand brushed my leg and I shivered. His entire body stilled as he looked up at me with some type of realization I didn't understand. My toes curled as he stepped closer to me and ran his nose along my collar bone.

"Fuck," he mumbled.

"What?" I asked seriously.

"You're just starting to go into heat with your birthday so close," he groaned and held me close. "It will be really... interesting when it fully sets in."

"What's heat?" I frowned, "Isn't that for animals?"

"Yes," he spoke softly, "or shifters. We don't know what you are, so I have no idea how this will work, we need to work on that today..."

His hands smoothed up my legs in a distracted fashion, his gaze outside and the movement had a hot rush flooding through me. A whimper came from my throat as his head snapped toward mine.

"Do you think you can go to sleep right now, honey?" He asked softly, his chest doing that odd rumbling again. My skin was prickling and I felt antsy, shifting slightly as my nipples tightened painfully. I felt my nails dig into his forearm slightly as his eyes darkened to nearly black.

I frowned, "I'm not sure, I feel very warm."

He nodded and pinned me with a look, "How bad is it?"

I didn't know what he was talking about but my body felt bad. I whispered, "Bad." I just knew that if he would touch me, it would fix some of this. I leaned forward into him.

Marco seemed to snap to some decision because he lifted my body up and walked the two of us towards the comfortable family room. I let out a small sound at the odd feeling of our pelvises connecting as I straddled him. He totally liked me also.

"What can I do to make it feel better?" He whispered, looking pained.

I shivered and pressed my body close to him, rolling my hips forward. I let out a whimper as his large hand floated from my hips to cupping my butt.

"Shit," he groaned softly. "Maya, honey, you need to

give me some direction here because I don't trust the direction I'd take."

My toes curled and I wiggled closer to him, my hips rocking on their own accord. Oh wow. I gasped as his hardness pressed against me, the apex of my thighs warm and wet. Marco continued to hold me close, but his other hand tilted my chin to look him in the eye.

"I'm going to do something and you tell me at any point to stop," he demanded softly. I was totally okay with that because let me tell you I had no idea what I was doing here. I just felt needy and my heart was going a million miles an hour. A fluttering like wings sounded from within me.

I nodded and he closed his eyes with a deep breath. It was like he was searching for some level of control. My eyes fluttered shut as his mouth met mine in the barest of kisses as his free hand grazed up my ribs and across my silk robe and shirt underneath. My breasts felt very tight and heavy as he teased the underneath of them. I wanted... I wanted him to touch me there. I took one of my hands and grasped his, stilling his movements. He deepened our kiss as I encouraged his hand to my very hard nipple.

"Please," I whispered as he hesitated. Something seemed to break then with him because my robe slipped off my shoulders and my silk tank nightgown straps began to slip down my arms.

"What do you need?" He asked, his voice deep and husky as hot kisses trailed my throat.

I let out a soft hiss as they trailed across my breast and neared my nipple. I was so frustrated, and a sound came from my throat I'd never heard myself make before as he chuckled in a dark, almost scary way. I found myself getting more excited as he nipped on the delicate skin.

Somewhere in the house a clock chimed, Friday at 2

am. I gasped as something pushed through me violently and Marco cursed and locked his arms around me. My whole center, from my throat down to between my thighs, lit up like a river of molten lava. I whimpered as the sound of wings bat in my ears and everything inside of me sparked dangerously.

"Marco," I whispered.

"Guess we got that wish," he muttered. "Shhhh, its okay, Maya. Just relax, I've got you."

I believed him, but it didn't stop the panic I felt when suddenly my chest exploded out to release six colorful flames that seemed to line the center of my sternum. I inhaled and immediately I realized what they'd meant about being mates.

It was like everything I knew became narrowed and these six massive planets started to circle around me. A sense of safety and love filtered through my chest, so overwhelming I started to feel like I'd drown. Fire licked under my skin as if branding me with their scent and I knew, without a doubt, their words had been true. I thought I had cared about them before, but it was nothing compared to the symphony of pure affection that emanated from inside of me now.

After a few moments, the feeling settled and I collapsed forward into Marco's arms. Everything stilled for a moment by breathing rough.

"Happy birthday, Maya," he whispered against my temple. My birthday? I had turned 18! Holy crap. I smiled because of everything that meant.

That flame of desire punched me right in the stomach and my head snapped up as those mint colored eyes darkened dangerously. A sound that he didn't mean to let out came from his throat.

"Maya..." He warned.

Hesitantly, but still feeling something oddly predatory inside of me, I leaned forward and pressed my lips to his. I knew Marco had been in control earlier, and he still could be, but I needed him to know that I wanted him, even if it just meant kissing.

"I'm 18," I reminded him.

He chuckled quietly and then groaned at my slight arch into him. "Honey, that was never a particular concern of mine, legal age of consent here is 16 for humans. On a mate perspective, I would have never taken anything too far unless you were 18 and very, very willing."

"I am very, very willing," I mumbled, not knowing if it was the thing to say as he hummed and this dominant edge flashed in his eyes.

I whimpered as his large hand came up to angle me back and hold my throat in a gentle, yet commanding way. My body shivered and I realized my tank top had fully slipped, exposing my breast that he began kissing his way down to.

"Oh wow," I whispered as his lips closed around my nipple. My legs began to shake as he gently tugged on them with his teeth and smoothed my hip with his other hand. I couldn't control my breathing and I found myself rolling into him, trying to grasp at something.

"Marco," I whispered in a pleading voice.

"I know what you need, sweet girl," he whispered as his large warm fingers pushed up my silk nightgown. I gasped as he touched my silk panties, causing a shock to go through me. My hips rolled as he groaned and I began breathing harsher.

"Maya," he whispered. "I need your attention."

I looked up at him as he spoke, "I'm going to take this

slow, but in order to do that, I need you to trust me and not try to rush anything. Alright?"

I nodded and his arm locked around my waist as a hot finger traced the edge of my panties. I wanted him to touch me there and... I wasn't positive what else, to be honest. I just needed his touch. My whimper was impossible to hide as he pulled my panties to the side before lightly running a finger where no one had ever touched me.

"You're so wet," he murmured, before popping a nipple into his mouth. "Have you ever touched yourself, Maya?"

My skin flushed as I spoke, "One time, when I was alone."

He hummed softly, "And how did you feel?"

"I think I did it wrong." I muttered on a soft moan into his neck as he straightened. "This feels much better."

He let out a curse, but began to swirl the pad of his finger over my nerve ending. I let out a soft sound as I felt wet heat turn molten between my legs. I felt my walls clench and as if he knew, Marco moved his fingers to my small, tight chanel. He slipped one finger in and I let out a soft needy moan.

"Honey," he groaned in a throaty sound. "Your little pussy is so tight."

"Marco," I whispered, "I need..."

His lips plastered to mine as his movements increased with speed until my legs were trembling and skin had broken into a flush. I let out a small cry as he continued to slide in and out of me and my eyes fluttered, causing him to grip me tighter.

My center began to tighten and his rough words caused molten heat to explode in my center.

"That's it, Sweetheart, are you going to cum on my fingers?"

If that was what this was leading to, *absolutely*. I whimpered out a half 'yes' and then his freakin' teeth pulled my nipple, causing me to gasp and tighten around him. I was moving on my own accord now, searching for the thing I knew would make me feel better. My hands wove into his thick dark hair as something inside of me just breathed out the word *'mate'*.

My lips pressed against his throat and when he increased his speed, I cried out his name. Exploding on his fingers as possibly the best feeling in the world, consumed me. A euphoric like high clouded my vision and his name was gasped from my mouth before I bit down on his neck, causing him to let out a low, pained noise. I couldn't help it though, it felt right and the shiver that overtook me had everything inside of me slumping in relief.

That.

That is what I needed.

"Oh wow," I whispered licking the bite mark I'd left. Marco was very still and when he turned his head and pulled his fingers from me, I could practically see his dragon looking back at me. His arm locked around me as he pressed his forehead against my own, causing me to melt.

"You marked me," he noted, his voice rough.

My eyes flew open as my mouth popped open in surprise. "I'm so sorry, Marco."

No idea what I was apologizing for.

He shook his head, looking way too serious. "Do not apologize for it, Maya, but tell me you meant it. You want to be my mate?"

A blush crawled on my cheeks. "Well, yeah. I mean, I thought I'd made that bit clear here."

Marco chuckled quietly before running his nose along my shoulder gently. "Can I mark you?"

His voice was so throaty and low, but this felt like it should be announced loudly. It seemed like a big deal. I considered it for a moment and realized I trusted Marco. I trusted them all. If he thought it was a good idea, then it probably was. The man could have easily taken advantage of how naive I was, and still am, yet he just continued to lead me through it, step by step.

"Yes," I whispered nodding.

"You know this seals the mating bond, right?" He whispers. See what I mean? "The others will want to mark you, but this will seal it for our entire flight for the time being, are you sure you want that? Want us?"

"Yes."

It was clear and loud. Just like my cry as his teeth, which seemed a lot flippin' pointer than before, broke my skin. He pulled back and his lips were stained with red as he licked it and his eyes closed. I could feel our connection tightening and my shoulder pulsed with warmth.

"Holy shit," Marco muttered, "Henry was right."

"What?" I frowned. The man in front of me adjusted my outfit and drew my robe up so I was comfortably dressed.

"You're a..." Right then a bell rang and Marco froze. I heard movement upstairs and Atlas was there in a second, his eyes dark.

"South border," he murmured.

Marco grunted and looked at me. "Maya, honey, can you go upstairs? Someone is trying to get onto our property and that most likely doesn't bode well. For them, at least."

I stood up and after a brief kiss, went to go watch from upstairs. Of course I'd watch. I had to make sure nothing bad happened to them. Atlas paused me and moved my hair looking at the bite mark as I shivered. My heart beat an unsteady rhythm as he flashed a smile.

"Early birthday?" He grinned as I nodded.

"Happy birthday." He pressed his lips to mine in a fleeting movement before my dragons were going outside. I frowned, feeling off about this entire thing and was glad to see a few of them stayed in the backyard. I could be tough, but defending an entire house on my own was a big stretch. I reached the top of the stairs and went towards my bedroom.

When my hair was tugged back and a cloth came over my mouth, I cursed out loud. I felt like it was well deserved, considering I blacked out looking up at Jed's furious eyes.

14

MAYA

"I should have known you were a whore this entire time."

Those were the first words that came out of my mother's mouth and the first I heard when I woke up from being knocked out. Heavy rope had me tied to the bed I was on, face down, and I could feel that only my tiny silk underwear remained. A panicked breath stole out of me because this was what I'd been afraid of. This was what Jed had represented to me.

"Are you listening girl?" My mother's voice echoed as I cried out and she ripped my hair back. Jed's large gross form rested against the wall, his eyes flickering down to my bare breasts. I nearly snarled at that.

"Are you?!" She screamed as I whimpered.

"Yes," I rasped out.

"Good." She dropped my hair and put out a hand as Jed undid his belt.

"Mom," I whimpered, "please don't."

Tears were coming heavy now. Tears of anticipation

because I knew this was going to hurt. I shook as she sneered at me. Her face level with mine.

"Jed told me he saw you fucking around with one of those boys," she hissed. "It made me realize he'd been right all along. You are a whore. So after this beating, I'm sending you off to work at one of Jed's clubs. The same fucking clubs that are paying for you to go to that bullshit school."

If she thought it was BS, why was she sending me there?

"It's either that or you can call Mr. Moretti yourself and ask for money from him." That sounds like the real reason. So had the two of them expected me to meet Henry and the twins?

"I'll call," I whispered hoping then he could figure out where I was at. Marco would be able to figure it out. Jed held up a flashlight as a little red light blinked on his cam recorder, I cringed into the mattress feeling horrible.

"We will see if you'll be able to call after this." My mother chuckled.

I think I knew this was going to be bad. Far worse than usual.

I cried out as the first lash hit me and I pulled against the ropes trying to curl in on myself. How did it still hurt so much? My sobs grew louder as she hit again and again. I could hear Jed fueling her anger and I was trembling as blood soaked the bed underneath me.

Then they started to fight.

Something about hurting me too much to do my job. She kept hitting me and my tears ran dry as this hazy odd feeling came over me. My eyes fluttered as I began to see black spots that clouded my vision. My mother's lashes were brutal and then she had her other hand on my neck, crushing it from the back and pushing me into the mattress.

I could barely breathe. The pulsing from the mating bite Marco had left on me was the only thing I could feel.

I whispered his name as my mother's hand tightened.

I realized then that I was going to die.

I'd never given much thought to dying. Honestly, I figured it would happen eventually, probably just like this. So when the reality of it hit me square in the face, all I felt was gratitude for these memories that were streaming through me like wildfire. This past week had been amazing.

There was a time before that as well. A time when a woman with the same colored eyes as me stared at me with love and affection. I missed those memories even though they were barely at the edge of my consciousness.

I knew I was going to die and when I breathed in my last breath, my back numb as blood splattered around me with the screams of their fight, I smiled.

At least I'd die knowing that everyone wasn't like this.

That was when everything faded to black.

15

MARCO

The mixture of pure terror and fury was an intoxicating mind numbing time stopping effect. The basement door of the rental house Jed owned flew towards the man, knocking him into the wall and skewering him as wood pushed through his chest. His cry went on empty ears though because the room around us shook as I realized my magic had exploded out.

Maya.

The feral woman continued to hit her and I tossed her to the side with ease, hearing bones crunch as the others, I hoped, went to take care of them. I dropped to my knees and felt terror slice through me.

No.

No.

No.

Absolutely fucking not.

My chest constricted and my dragon pushed at my skin as I tried to undo her wrists. Her little golden face was pressed to the side and her back was shredded to pieces. Her throat had bruising. I snapped the leg restraints and lifted her into my arms off the bed where I knelt on the floor. She wasn't breathing. Her face was a tinge of blue and her blood soaked my dress shirt.

"Maya, honey," I whispered, knowing it was useless but not caring. My heart began to slow and I realized that the fracture in my chest, the cavern where my heart used to be, was void without her. Void and breaking. Shattering at the very real fact that Maya was…

Dead.

For the first time in my life, tears pricked my eyes and not even the sounds of the two pieces of shit dying made me feel better. Instead, I buried my head in her neck and quietly asked her to wake up. Again. And again. After a few moments or hours, I realized the room had filled with an icy silence. My breathing was rough as I pulled back and I didn't need to look around to feel the absolute heartbreak that filled the room. No one knew what to do.

My eyes closed as a single tear dropped off my chin and my dragon let out a low pained sound.

The drop landed on her skin and the sound of sizzling had my eyes snapping open.

Maya's neck was turned, but where my tear had slid down, her skin began to shimmer in a scale like pattern. I could feel the others shift closer but I couldn't bear to look up at them. My eyes widened slightly as a fine fissure, almost like lava, cracked the center of her chest and sent the painful sound through the room. Henry's hand on my shoulder had me laying her down on the ground.

Right in time because, from that center crack, her entire form lit up.

I mean truly became a live wire of open gasoline flames that wrapped around her body and turned her skin a charred ash. I cringed as her body shook and I felt as though I had to be hallucinating.

"She's being reborn," Henry said softly with a bit of awe his glassy eyes. I looked back and watched as the inferno soared with color and shades of reds, yellows, and oranges hitting the ceiling and spread out around the room, burning everything but us. My eyes refused to stray from her though and the flames grew so thick I couldn't see her form for a moment, the tiny bit of hope I had was backing away.

Then the flames retreated and my eyes widened at the unconscious form of our mate.

I leaned forward, resting my jacket across her, and cupping her jaw. Her pulse was strong and vibrant, the smile on her face nearly serene. She looked completely untouched.

"She's alive," I choked out.

"She's a fucking pheonix," Henry added, his voice completely blank.

That was accurate, but I didn't care about that right now. I leaned forward and picked her up gently as her little brow furrowed. I watched as those stunning, chocolate brown eyes littered with gold flecks opened and pinned me with a wide eyed expression.

"Marco?" She whispered her voice clear as a bell. I wasn't positive what had caused the raspy nature of it before, but that was gone. Completely.

"Maya," I murmured.

Her eyes flickered around as she sat up and looked down at her body. Then she met everyone's gaze looking absolutely in shock. Tears welled up in her eyes.

"Holy shit. I'm alive."

Thank fucking god.

The midmorning light filtered through the sitting room as I leaned back trying to detox from whatever the fuck that had been this morning. She had barely been out of my sight for a fucking hour or two and she'd died.

Actually died.

I had immediately called the contractors to come install a better security system after we had a shifter doctor come by to make sure she was okay. Despite it being Friday and her birthday, I felt like I needed a fucking nap. I had to thank small blessings though because she'd been tired, but seemed far better than I'd expected. I also hated to admit how I loved that she clung to me a bit more than even before.

Atlas had been afraid to touch her afterwards because he'd essentially killed Jed with his bare hands. Normally, he would have had qualms with killing women, especially human, but her mother was very dead now. Sai had been all too pleased to help remove all evidence with the twins. The twins who seemed to have woven themselves around her once again upstairs, leaving just Henry and me in the living room. Drinking coffee and attempting to function.

And yes, I'd called the school to notify them of their absence today.

"So she's a phoenix," I noted.

Henry's eyes flashed over to her easel displaying a fire bird of sorts spiraling upwards. "Yes, I think that is fairly obvious now. Although, trying to get her to shift and convincing her is going to be a different story."

"I'm just glad we got her out of there and that they're dead," I murmured.

Henry's eyes flashed dangerously, "They deserved far more pain than that."

This was one of the reasons Henry was my chosen beta. He was smart, sure, but he also knew when to act like a leader and when it wasn't necessary. He also had a vicious mean streak he kept hidden, unlike Anani and Atlas. The two of them had no issue showcasing it. I tried to keep more level headed, but right now I could easily imagine killing a few dozen people. Or just Jed and her mother. Again and again.

"We need to try to give her time to rest this weekend," he commented.

I nodded, "We could head down to Los Angeles."

His lip twitched, "Wanting to take her around the dragon council now that she has your mark?"

I shrugged nonchalantly, "I think my fellow council men and women would do well to meet her."

But yes. That was exactly what it was fucking about. I wanted to show her off to everyone. Take her to every single red carpet event for humans and anything within the shifter community. Just so everyone knew whose mate she was. I didn't want or need any fucking confusion.

Henry hummed and nodded, "I'll arrange for the jet, when do you want to leave?"

"This afternoon," I stated, "once she wakes up, and if she doesn't, she can wake up there and I'll let her sleep through the plane ride."

He offered a two finger salute and headed upstairs. I leaned back into the leather and looked at my blood soaked shirt. I needed a fucking shower. Standing up, I unbuttoned my shirt and walked into my bedroom. It was neat and organized, severely lacking a beautiful little phoenix, but I didn't want to wake her up.

The shower was much needed and I was nearly in there for an hour, my head pressed against the tile wall. Stuck between being terrified of what had happened earlier, thankful she was alive, and turned on from the memory of her cumming on my fingers last night. Fucking shit. I knew she didn't know a lot about sex besides the basics, but the woman had a natural sexuality and beauty to her that was just essential to who she was. I muttered a curse as I started to get hard, but I had to shut that shit down. I was far too exhausted right now as it was.

I dried off my hair and pulled on a pair of shorts before walking back into my room.

My lips pressed together into a smile because my room looked exactly the same, except for the little ball of soft skin and dark hair curled up in the center of it. She really did remind me a bit of a kitten. Maybe, I'd get her a kitten as a late birthday present. Did she like kittens even? I'd have to ask. Her face was peaceful and it was hard to coordinate in my head the reality of this morning with now. I shook my head and slid into bed behind her, wrapped my arms tightly around her form. With an inhale and exhale, she relaxed into me completely.

The last thought I'd had before falling asleep was how perfect she felt in my arms.

16

MAYA

"This is a plane?" I asked, narrowing my eyes at the metal craft that was supposed to fly us down the coast.

"One of them," Sai tossed me a grin.

I raised a brow, "Why would you need more than one? This is huge."

Ledger kissed my head, "This isn't even a big one, this only fits ten people. We have an overseas one that can fit an entire press worth of people."

I shook my head and tucked my hands into my jacket. I had to admit for having died this morning, I felt pretty great. No really. My skin was flushed looking and my hair seemed extra silky. Even my eyes seemed brighter. Maybe I was just having a good day or something beauty wise. I had even picked out a cute outfit.

I wore these hot pink Hunter boots that kept my wool socked feet warm and out of the rain. My leggings were tight and lined, but a massive oversized Irish knit sweater covered my butt and kept me cozy along with my jacket and scarf. Atlas had put a hat on my head despite not feeling like I needed it, sort of thankful for it now considering the sprinkling of rain.

This morning in some ways felt unreal. As if, there was no way it had happened. Everyone was acting odd though. Maybe not odd, just very intense. Protective, yes, they were still hugging me and acting like they normally did. There was just an underlying change to the atmosphere. Henry seemed quieter as well, but his arms wrapped around me made me feel a lot better. Everytime I looked up at him, he had an intense expression despite his ears heating a bit.

I had never understood the mating bond, but holy crap, did I now.

I felt so... at peace. Before I felt comfortable and wanted, but this was like an anchor and I could feel my body relaxing as they almost adjusted to what they felt like I needed. I would bet I was doing the same in some instances. Marco was talking to the pilot and my cheeks pinkened slightly thinking about last night and I tried to tamper it. I didn't feel nearly as worked up as I had then but I could feel it simmering under the surface along with whatever had brought me back to life.

Henry was right. I wasn't human.

They said I was a phoenix and that didn't sound wrong. But it was overwhelming, all of this was. I had learned about the human world my entire life, but never had the opportunity to experience it. Then I got to experience it and I'm told that this world doesn't even apply to me! It was a lot for one woman to handle in less than a week.

Marco was dressed similar to Henry, both in casual button downs and pants with fitted jackets. They almost looked like the businessmen in the magazines and I wasn't positive why they were so dressed up. Then you had Ledger, who was wearing a hoodie and Anani that had this soft multi-colored shirt on that I kept rubbing between my fingers. Atlas had on a tan leather jacket and boots, while Sai wore a dark sweater and jeans, his hair still wet and styled back.

Gosh darn, they really were handsome.

Henry spoke quietly in my ear, "How are you feeling, Sweetheart?"

I looked up at him and smiled, "Thankful."

Wasn't that the truth? You would have thought I felt sad, angry, or guilty. I was just glad they were dead and that sounded cruel, but it was true. I knew that the situation had left an impact on me because I'd woken up in a cold sweat when I'd somehow rolled onto my stomach. A position that no doubt would be an issue for me for a bit.

Besides that though? I felt strong. I felt like I wasn't as scared anymore.

I still didn't think I was good enough for them, but if they wanted me around, I'd stay. I'm not sure I could leave with this crazy connection running through me. I had no idea where this was headed, but I woke up realizing that since I hadn't died, I was going to make the best of what I did have.

"Come on, Kitten." Sai nodded toward the jet and I strode forward with an excited gait. I smiled at the captain as he smiled back, until Anani growled at him. A little thrill in my chest had me smiling. I was starting to notice things about the boys I hadn't before.

Like they growled a lot.

They also weren't very friendly outside of our group. I paused and looked at Marco, his eyebrow hitching.

"I'm going to miss work," I stated softly, my tone was worried.

His eyes softened, "Already called her, said you can start Monday."

Awesome.

The jet was stunning. A long cabin that had a bar at the back with cream colored seats and a series of TV screens. I tucked my feet under me after taking off my boots and Atlas joined me, pulling me into his side slightly.

"What are you doing?" I asked him as I looked down from the news station to his laptop that was on the small table in front of us.

His eyes warmed on my face. "I am ensuring security is up to par at our LA property."

I nibbled my lip. "What is Los Angeles like?"

"Harder to fly in, less cloud cover, and more polluted," Ledger muttered.

"Shut it," Henry called.

"He's just upset, Peanut ," Anani chirped, "we have a bit of a reputation in LA and so we have to make an active effort to avoid the media."

I frowned and nodded. "Is this because of your business?"

"Amongst other things," Sai chuckles. I felt like I wasn't getting something here.

"Did anyone consider that?" Atlas spoke quietly, "The media is going to get wind of her and when they try to find public record..."

"It will be blank," Marco shrugged, "we just need to stay out of the limelight while we are here."

"Aww, I wanted her to see us sing," Anani whined.

"Sing?" I tilted my head.

"We have a band," Ledger grinned, tossing up this little squishy ball and catching it.

"You can't call it a band when you only do shows when

you're in town and they perform the rest of the time," Sai noted, rolling his eyes.

"I want to see you sing," I looked at both twins.

"Maya..." Marco spoke quietly.

"Please Marco," I looked at him earnestly.

He examined my face and muttered, "Fine. Private show at the house, minimum invites, we can use it as an introduction for the dragon council."

"What's the dragon council?" I chirped.

"Marco serves on the board," Henry noted, "our realm is a bit... archaic. So many of our kind moved here and have been living quietly. You can consider it a political ruling class of sorts. There are five council members."

My eyes went back to Marco's, "So... you're like super important."

Atlas chuckled. "Don't stroke his ego, Angel."

Marco snorted but then the plane started to go faster after moving around the little airport. I turned on my butt and looked out the window, my eyes taking in the cloudy atmosphere. A low engine buzzing was the only thing to prepare me before Atlas snapped a belt around my waist. I barely paid attention because it started moving.

Fast.

Faster.

I grinned as suddenly the earth dropped out from under us and we angled up. An excited hum came from my mouth as I pressed my cheek to the window trying to see more. I felt my ears pop slightly as we move up and up, as something settles deep in my chest.

"Firefly?" Ledger asked and I just keep watching. I inhaled and smiled as we broke above the clouds.

"Holy shit. I mean crap." I muttered.

"You've flown on my dragon before, Kitten," Sai muttered scowling.

I giggled, "This is different, *you* make sense. This big old metal thing in the air doesn't."

My body sunk back slightly as Atlas ran his hand through my hair. I kept my eyes on the sky and after a few minutes my eyes fluttered shut and I ended up falling asleep.

17
ATLAS

"This is a bad idea," I stated simply as we began our departure. It was only about an hour flight but we had to circle the airport a few times since we were going into the larger LA airport. My security team had already let me know the media had been informed of our arrival. This was why we fucking stayed in Washington.

Henry interrupted me momentarily by raising the volume on the news. The stock market was about to close for the day an excited look came over our betas face and he stood, pointing at one of the companies running in the banner.

"Do you fucking see that Marco?" Henry grinned. "What did I tell you? Didn't I tell you this was going to be their week?"

Henry really, really, *really* liked investing. I muttered a curse to myself as Maya shifted, I really needed her to keep sleeping so that she was more well rested. I worried about her. You know, considering she fucking died less than 12 hours ago.

"I know," Marco grinned watching the screen. "I believed you enough to buy shares in it, didn't I?"

"How much did it go up?" Sai asked, aimlessly wandering the cabin.

Henry opened his tablet, "For our share? Like a few hundred thousand per share. No big deal *but* it is nice to know my program worked."

I frowned thinking about how the negative aspect of money was how much we had to fucking worry about people paying attention to Maya.

"We will be fine. I would never let anything happen to her," Marco stated, finally answering my question as I looked down at her little sleeping face. Her lashes fluttered with turbulence so I shifted her slightly. She sat up rolling her shoulders back and pushing those perky fucking breasts out while stretching. My eyes traced her slender neck and that mating mark made me fucking groan.

I was wondering how long it would be until the mating heat hit her hard and I was hoping it would be prolonged for a bit. I just didn't think she was ready for that completely. I would love to tell you that I was strong enough to resist her, but if Maya crawled onto my lap and asked me to fuck her, I would. In a fucking heart beat. I didn't think any of us were strong enough to not give her what she asked for, let alone that. Maya turned and met my gaze, her eyes hooded slightly as my lips tilted up. I'd felt protective over her from the start but this morning had really changed something.

My dragon felt semi-sated after he broke both of their necks. Well, *we* did. It wasn't enough though, and trying to push it under my skin wasn't boding very well. The only thing that was helpful was that she was so relaxed and calm. I could tell she authentically felt peaceful and I worried about how she was dealing with this so well. It didn't seem natural. Still, on some level, I had to trust her.

But the bad idea aspect of today?

The media. I did not, I repeat, *did not* want her in the eyes of the media. She spoke softly, pulling me out of it, "you look sad, why?"

"Not sad." I rubbed a thumb over her cheekbone. "Just concerned. You are going to have a lot of pictures being taken of you here in a moment."

She nibbled her lip, "Is that bad?"

"No." I shook my head. "I just don't like the security threat it poses."

She climbed on my lap, her eyes intelligent and bright. The woman was a magnet and I felt like she moved a million miles an hour. I was selfish and I didn't want to share her. Maya licked her lips subconsciously. "Don't worry, Atlas, we've got this." I loved hearing the word *we* from her mouth because it made me know she was accepting this bond.

The plane landed as I locked my hands around her and she laughed at the bounce. My eyes immediately shot to the line of media against the fence of the private airport. Everyone started shifting as Maya pulled on her shoes and I helped her tuck this cute purple hat around her ears. She blushed a bit and I nearly shook my head, I still wasn't sure how it was possible for someone to be equally adorable and sexy at the same time.

My brain immediately flashed to her in that lace pair of panties with a fucking bow in the back. I would love to unwrap that present.

"She's going to be warm," Ledger pointed out and I nodded.

"It's chillier than normal but we can change once we get

to the house," I muttered. She stood and when the plane came to a stop, I grasped her hand in mine and led her to the door. Marco offered me a look that was meant to be reassuring, but I still wasn't positive. This entire thing, having her this exposed, made me nervous as hell. I know he said it wasn't about that and this was more about relaxing. But I still didn't like it.

What was wrong with relaxing at our house?

Or never leaving her fucking bedroom?

As soon as we stepped out, the cameras and voices started. You have to understand, me founding a security company wasn't out of interest. It was a necessity. Marco's business had boomed, and along with that, the twins were usually swarmed with people. Add on Henry's young, record breaking, medical career and Sai's fighting, and we were a bit of a known thing. I watched Maya, and instead of looking nervous, her lips pressed into a surprised smile. Marco had a hand on her lower back as they walked next to one another.

I knew in the eye of the public, they'd be a couple. That didn't bother me, *no* actually it did. It did bother me because she was mine also. Dragons were complicated like that, possessive despite knowing they had to share.

Almost as if knowing what I was thinking, Maya looked back at me and flashed a smile, offering a hand. I met Marco's gaze and the boy I'd first become best friends with, was there with an amused grin. He shrugged and I shook my head, taking her hand as people over the fence flipped. I could practically hear the 5 o'clock news already.

"Maya," I spoke, "Humans are a bit different with their relationships."

She laughed softly, "You mean having six mates isn't standard?"

Now that sassy tone was just fucking unfair, my entire body hardened at that and I was finding out little Maya had more than a bit of fire. She adapted so quickly and that could only mean she would adjust to the twin's sarcasm and our intensity, something I loved. It was like we were leaving an imprint on her while she still managed to maintain her sweetness and strength.

"They are going to talk, honey," Marco spoke softly, although he didn't look like he gave a fuck.

Then she just fucked with my head as she hopped in the car. "They can talk all they want, last time I checked they weren't on planes with their six handsome mates. So, their loss."

Marco laughed and I shook my head, her point was valid.

Our drive was pretty straightforward and while paparazzi followed alongside us, Maya gave zero mind, instead shedding her jacket and looking over the Los Angeles streets with interest. I tucked her jacket away and as we approached a set of massive white gates that rose in greeting, she moved forward to kneel on the seat and watch.

That was one of the things I appreciated most about the woman.

Her pure curiosity and interest for things. It was nearing sunset, so the sky was painted a stunning hue of red and purple, as we pulled around the circular driveway to the massive Grecian styled architecture that faced the ocean, Maya was out. She had a huge smile on her face as the twins caught up to her and they walked right through the foyer, past the massive staircase and elaborate classic furniture, towards the private beach and balcony. The gauzy white curtain shifted as she stood outlined in them, looking over the ocean.

I looked to Marco and spoke, "I'm starting to think this house was a good purchase."

Marco's eyes snapped back to her as he replied, "I think this house was bought for her whether we realized it or not."

It was true, only minutes later, Maya had found her way upstairs and changed into a sundress. I'd opted for a shirt and shorts as well but I didn't feel nearly as relaxed as she looked. I could literally see the men I had lining the property, but it didn't help, and Marco, despite his words was a tad tense, the two of us smoking cigars in the oddly cool LA afternoon. Yes, 70 degrees was cool for here.

The twins were walking along the shore line with Maya, and Sai was setting up a bonfire. Henry stood talking on the phone as he made arrangements for tomorrow night.

"I'm surprised you said yes to the concert," I noted.

Marco snorted and looked away from Maya's long dark hair that was moving like her dress in the breeze. Barefoot, the pastel blue dress with a bow on the back was the only color on the shoreline along side the twins. I could hear her laugh from here and it was like this morning had never happened. But it had. Which was why I was starting to be really thankful for the level of security I had available. I get it. Jed was dead. I didn't give a fuck, there were other threats and I wasn't about to let them touch her.

"I think," Marco blew out shaking his head, "that I would do anything for that woman."

I nodded and drew a hand through my hair, my dragon rumbling in agreeance. I wondered if she'd ever realize the power she had over us.

Whatever the woman wanted, I'd gladly hand over to her and ten times that.

18

MAYA

"I have never been to the beach," I explained, "I didn't expect it to be so cold."

"Isn't always," Anani grinned. "Peanut, you should visit the Bahamas or Fiji. You would love that."

Ledger nodded and tucked a piece of hair behind my ear, "I agree. I like you in the sunshine, you look like you're glowing. Maybe we need to move down here."

"I like both," I pointed out because it was true. Living in the damp foggy weather made me appreciate this more and vice versa.

I turned in the sand to look back at the massive columned architecture that sat in front of me. I couldn't even see in detail the closest house, but I could see my other mates. Sai sat on a log by the bonfire and I walked over to him, ignoring the twins asking where I was going. Instead of saying anything, I dropped down right into his lap. Sai grunted and then laughed, his arms tightening around me.

"Hey Kitten," he purred.

I stretched and looked at the bonfire, my chest warming, "I like this."

"I like you." He nibbled on my throat, making me squeak as I felt my skin break out into shivers. That low simmering boil under my skin was pushing me to move closer to him. To rub against him more. I also really wanted to see it again. I wanted to confirm size, folks. Didn't curiosity kill the cat?

"That is a dangerous look," he purred, pulling me so I was straddling him, leaning back in the sand as my hair created a veil over us. We ended up like this a lot with me on top of him.

"What look?" I blinked because I really had no idea what they meant by that.

"It's a look that makes me want to devour those sweet lips," he drawled lazily as my cheeks flamed.

"Well, maybe I want you to do that," I squeaked, feeling a little less nervous than before.

Sai let out a low hum and grasped my jaw, gently pulling me down. I shivered as his lips pressed to mine, right before I was taken from his arms. Henry shook his head, carrying me towards the balcony.

"Henry!" Sai chuckled in legitimate surprise.

"Photos Sai, I don't want photos in the media," he shouted back. I was already distracted and very happy. My hands gripped Henry's button down as I stared at the buttons. I could undo them. I just wanted more access to his skin.

"Behave," he whispered, walking up the stairs.

"I am," I flashed a smile as his eyes glinted behind his glasses.

"If this is behaving, it sounds like you may need a lesson in it," he murmured.

"Yeah?" I nibbled my lip, knowing this was flirting and hoping I was sort of good at it. "And would you teach me that?"

Henry let out a low noise and narrowed his eyes, "I could teach you a whole lot, Maya, but be careful what you ask for."

Before I could ask what that meant, he'd placed me down and I turned to face Marco and Atlas. The latter was smoking what I thought was a cigar and had that damn laptop in front of him. Marco had sunglasses on and a cigar in his mouth, jacket thrown over his chair. I nibbled my lip and approached him. I wasn't positive what it was about how he looked right now, but it made my center tighten like last night. He took off his glasses as his eyes lit up and he patted one of his knees, I adjusted my skirt and sat right on his knee, looking eye to eye with him.

"Are you hungry?" He asked, his eyes searching my face.

"Always am," I noted because that was accurate.

His smile was authentic as he nodded and Henry, who'd been watching me still, ducked into the house. I leaned against Marco's chest and watched the twins tossed a ball back and forth as Sai chatted aimlessly with them. A sigh of contentment filled me.

This was something special.

I have no idea how much later it was, but at some point food was set on the table in front of me along with beverages and I raised my brows. That was a lot of freakin' food.

"I don't know where to start," I mumbled as Marco reached over and created a small plate, putting it in front of us.

I reached for one of the cheese cubes, but he just grabbed my hand and kissed the top of it. Then in a move that had me shivering, he pressed a thumb to my lips, making them pop open. He placed a cheese cube in my mouth and I squeaked as flavor exploded on my tongue. He grinned and I savored the taste, because when you ate PB&J sandwiches most of your life, you savored the small things.

Henry, at some point, joined us at the table as they started talking about the event tomorrow night but Marco didn't let me move a finger. I was sipping on lemonade, leaning into him when a phone pinged on the table, causing all of us to startle. Anani muttered a curse and opened it.

"It is exactly as bad as we assumed," he stated and put it down.

My smile grew as I leaned forward and saw that Marco and Atlas were on either side of me smiling about something. I didn't even care about the headline that said something about 'sharing'.

"Can you print that picture out?" I chirped.

Ledger chuckled as Anani pressed a kiss to my forehead. It was cute, *sorry not sorry*.

"We need more pictures," Henry notes thoughtfully, "the media will be asking and I would rather they be on our terms."

"We need to talk about how we want to handle this," Marco spoke carefully and then aimed it at me, "would you feel more comfortable telling the humans you were with one of us…"

"No," I scowled, "I am not going to lie. The truth is I am mates with all of you and I would rather just tell them that then get in trouble for lying."

The entire table seemed to freeze and I wasn't positive what I'd said but Sai broke into a huge grin. "You know, Kitten, if you weren't already my mate, I'd probably be down on one knee right now."

"Does your knee hurt?" I raised a brow.

For some reason that made everyone laugh. I wasn't positive what I'd done that was so funny.

"It's just wine," Anani grinned, "she's fine."

"It's not about that," Henry stated.

I grinned sitting around the bonfire as Anani handed me a clear glass of sparkly wine. Well, they called it champagne, but it seemed to be the same thing. I sipped it gently and taste exploded on my tongue as I hummed. My toes were warm and cozy in the sand.

It was just the three of us down here right now and the soft sound of the ocean lapping was relaxing. A shawl was wrapped around my shoulders and Henry continued to sooth my hair with his large warm hands.

Something occurred to me as I watched the fire.

"If I am a shifter," I note softly, taking another sip, "why haven't I shifted?"

Henry hummed with interest, "well, with some species it happens automatically. From what I've learned about phoenix lore so far, it seems that you have to instigate the process and draw your creature out."

"How the heck am I supposed to do that?" I muttered as Anani laughed.

He spoke then, "try closing your eyes and reaching for... well, I'm not sure what it would be for you."

"Remember the flame you told me about?" Henry asked softly. "Try that."

I closed my eyes and inhaled. Right at my center, six flames burned around a black lick of fire. I tried to pull on it, but it seemed to almost watch me with a lazy indifference. I frowned and tried to pull harder, but all it did was seem to make her sink lower into the center of them.

Alright then.

My eyes fluttered open. "She doesn't want to work with me."

"She?" Henry grinned.

"Yes she," I mumbled, "I blame your magic though because she's surrounded by your six flames and refusing to move."

Anani barked out a laugh, "How is that our fault?"

I finished my glass and held out my glass for more, "The bubbly queen requests more."

Henry warned, "Anani."

"It was a royal decree," Anani grinned, "plus this is the bottom of the bottle anyway."

I hummed and drank it down as I leaned back into Henry, Anani taking the bottle upstairs. My blonde dragon kissed the top of my head gently.

"What are you thinking about?" He asked.

I sipped the drink and looked up at him, "Honestly? Nothing really. Just loving this."

He hummed and strummed my throat gently. "How are you feeling after today?"

I sat up and squeezed his hand, "Henry, I promise you, I'm fine."

I thought I had been. I was wrong.

I had no idea that was the case though until about two hours later. I'd walked barefoot up to the house with Henry and fell right into a bed. No idea whose bed but I felt safe as the breeze brushed through the room. The moment my eyes closed I knew it was going to be an issue.

My face was hit with a cool fresh wind that seemed to taste different than the air around here. I let my shoulders pull back as feathers brushing broke in my ears. A caw-like sound had me smiling as I dived down only seeing a thick cloudy earth. There was a warmth and the sight of red right beyond my line of sight. It was beautiful.

Everything for just a moment seemed suspended and perfect.

Something slammed into me so hard that my seemingly large wings broke and I cried out falling towards the ground. Or what I hoped wouldn't be my death. A laugh taunted me as I fell and fell. Someone whispered soft in my ear.

I've got you.

They clearly hadn't. I screamed as memories crawled past me. I saw my mother's face. Pastor Malcolm. A flash of familiar eyes. I could feel my head pounding and my throat was raw. I had no idea how long I fell, but when I finally hit bottom, my neck snapped back and I let out a scream.

Jed was there with my mother holding me down. My face hit the ground as lashes began to break apart my back.

Again.

And again.

And again.

A bubble of panic wore through me and I felt as though if I died this time I wouldn't come back. My voice produced a high note and everything, all the images around me, shattered like glass.

My eyes snapped open and I gasped finding a pair of warm blue eyes filling my vision. Ledger.

"Maya." He was shaking me and I realized tears were streaking my cheeks. A soothing chest against my back had my heart rate slowing as I trembled. I couldn't detach from the dream completely and it was making me feel disoriented and detached from this reality.

"Firefly," Ledger spoke in a soothing tone, "you're okay."

"I know," I whispered in a raspy voice. "I know."

"What happened?" He asked quietly, the streaks of orange in his hair looking nearly red.

The dream was fading though, the only memorable part was of my mother holding me down. I shook my head and curled into Henry, feeling overwhelmed. Instead of answering, I fell back asleep.

19
HENRY

Maya fell immediately back to sleep and I watched as tears streamed down her face still. Ledger offered me a concerned look and I just shook my head. It hadn't been crying that had woken us. No, it was the high pitched noise that had come from her throat before turning into sobs. My dragon had practically forced a shift from the panicked noise and now there was no fucking way I'd be falling asleep. With careful movements, I shifted her so she was pressed into Ledger and stood.

Despite not shifting, I was almost 100% positive she was a phoenix. If she wasn't, I had no idea what she could possibly be. What I needed was to talk to someone who knew more about that lore than I did. I walked into my room and got into the shower, nearly 5am and my day was already starting, no doubt creating a map forward on how busy I'd be.

Not only were we hosting an event here tonight, but the politics behind the dragon council being here were touchy.

Once fully dressed in a suit and walking downstairs, I

picked up my phone to call the only person I assume would know anything about this. Croy Lee.

"Henry," his southern accent drawled, "what can I do for you?"

I had no idea when the man slept because everytime I called him, despite living right here in LA, he was awake. He worked closely as a scholar for the dragon council, but was a wolf shifter who had separated from his own pack.

"Are you available to come over this morning?"

"I'm assuming you aren't in Washington?"

I chuckled, "You would be right."

"How does 15 minutes sound?"

"Perfect, be sure to bring everything you have on shifter lore."

He hung up and I really hadn't needed to remind him, it was somewhat impossible for him to forget anything because he had the entire files not only in his head, but on his computer. Despite having entertained myself with a stint in medical school, only finally gaining my license once turning eighteen, my real passion had been focusing on the computer system he and I had developed. One that Microsoft and Apple had been trying to buy out for two years now.

By the way, yes, the only reason I was in high school, or pretending to be, was to keep an eye on the twins. I'd been able to complete medical school at a local university in the evenings while still attending high school during the day. I didn't want to consider what that said about the workload at both Earth realm institutions.

Although, now that Maya was in the picture, I was grateful for the lie about high school.

If Washington was our sanctuary where we could act like humans, this was the limelight. Our estate staff were already prepping for the event outback and the media lined up outside. I couldn't blame them, we were interesting and Maya had made 5 o'clock news. I smiled, thinking about how stunning she looked walking around this place like her cute little butt owned it. She *did* for the record, as of this morning our lawyers were adding her to everything.

I must have been lost in my thoughts for a bit because the roar of a Lamborghini had me slipping on sunglasses to step outside. Croy was a large guy and I had no idea why he insisted on such a small fucking car. He flashed the media a wave and walked up the steps, meeting my handshake as we walked back inside to find Marco already dressed and in the living room with the newspaper and coffee. Not unusual for before 8, but then again, I didn't think he'd been sleeping well lately.

"Croy," Marco noted, "good to see you."

"You as well," Croy drawled, his Alabamian accent thick as he lounged on the couch before slipping out his laptop. I sat in an armchair and tried to figure out a way to ask him to look up phoenix lore. Marco hadn't asked why he was here, so if I had to guess, he'd assumed.

"So what lore information do you need?"

"What do you know about phoenix lore?" I tried to act relaxed but Croy's raised eyebrows had me stilling. He put the laptop to the side and leaned forward, grabbing the coffee that had been brought out to him.

"Why the hell do you want to know about them?" He chuckled as my dragon threatened to make a defensive noise.

"Croy," I offered him a dry look.

He ran a hand through his hair. "Alright, well essentially, phoenixes themselves are a bit different than your average shifter and unique enough that I don't even need to look this up for you. First, until they reach 18, the only real magic they possess is the ability to regenerate and past 18, they have to be the one to instigate any shift, usually through high emotions or frustration."

So I was at least accurate about that.

"In terms of dragon lore, phoenixes are said to be the only true mates to dragons."

"What?" Marco asked, tilting his head.

"Well, you're species doesn't have females, right? So any females you do mate with are usually producing shifters that are only part dragon or not at all. Phoenixes can produce pure blood dragon sons, and daughters who are phoenixes."

Shit.

"So they are prized after?" Marco summarized and I knew he was concerned about the dragon council.

"Highly, considering we haven't had any in hundreds of years. Puritan religious cults killed most of them off by draining their blood, believing the regenerative qualities were the same as that brought their Jesus Christ back to life or something like that. The concept became particularly popular during World War II when the Nazis were rumored to be looking for the Holy Grail and other religious items. You know humans, always looking for some type of immortality. They believed, and passed down the belief that phoenixes were the Holy Grail of creatures, so of course like the destructive creatures they are, humans killed them off. Their blood, for the record, does not help humans at all. Or at least, hasn't been shown to."

Oh shit.

"They use to try to do it when they were younger, weaker, and sometimes it worked, sometimes not. Some would even just be reborn again and again under that torture. No one has found if there is a true way to kill a phoenix. When they stopped being reborn, the natural assumption was that they died. I'd imagine though, it was something different, after all they are considered the greatest survivors within the supe world."

"I bet that the 'baptism' she mentioned was their first attempt," I blurted out at Marco, thinking about how she said she'd burnt off the water during her baptism. Her mother must have killed her and she regenerated. *This was so fucked up.*

Croy went to ask what I was talking about when a soft voice chimed. A voice that was all Maya, but void of the vocal injury she used to have.

"Does that mean she tried to kill me that first time?"

Smart, brilliant Maya. My head snapped around to find her standing on the grand staircase foyer looking into the sitting room with just an oversized shirt and soft robe, her thick dark hair laying in waves around her head like a little halo. I was so caught up on how beautiful she looked that my response times were slowed. Several things happened at once.

A growl ripped from Croy's chest and Marco tried to move to block her from him, but the wolf shifter had her pinned in a blink of an eye. I growled, jumping over the back of the couch and reaching them, where she was against the staircase with him leaning over her. At first, I was really hating that we were going to have to kill such a useful person, but then I placed a hand on Marco's shoulder to stop him from moving forward.

Maya was completely and utterly unfazed by Croy.

Instead, she laid a hand on his chest that was producing a rumble and offered him a small smile. I watched in horror as Croy leaned forward to run his nose along her neck and she just seemed to completely relax, a bright pink blush hitting her cheeks. What the fuck was going on here?

"You're a wolf?" She asked curiously as her voice seemed to snap Croy out of it, causing him to step back and mutter a curse. I'd seen the man experience a lot of different emotions but this? Never.

"Yeah," he whispered, his throat still producing that sound.

"Neat." She flashed a smile and walked past him toward the living room, picking up Marco's coffee and curling up in the seat there. The three of us were still frozen.

"What the fuck was that Croy?" Marco was nearly vibrating with energy. It goes without saying, Croy was close, without being family. We didn't let many people into our house outside of events. Outside of our flight he was probably one of the closest friends we had, but I could see Marco was not only confused but territorial.

Croy pinned him with a look, his eyes nearly black. "I could ask you the same fucking thing. Why is my mate here with you?"

You've got to be fucking joking.

20

MAYA

The man was an absolute teddy bear.

He was huge, like Atlas big, and had his really pretty tan skin and honey blonde hair that laid sort of messy over a pair of dark green eyes. I could hear his wolf right under the surface and while I was on Marco's lap, my magic was running loops around Henry and Croy.

I liked the name Croy.

"Maya," Croy drawled, his accent reminding me of a similar one from where I'd grown up.

"Yes?" I asked, looking up from the newspaper.

"I don't even know where to start," he muttered his accent thicker while looking at Henry. Henry who was staring at me with an odd mixture of heat and concern. How did I know it was heat? He kept giving me that look whenever he wanted to kiss me. Don't ask me how I knew he wanted to kiss me. I could just tell he did. My eyes went back down to the story headline about some political candidate for the upcoming election.

Hm. I sort of wanted to vote.

I also wanted more kisses and more of whatever the

heck Marco did to me. Where Sai's kisses tasted like cinnamon and had my heart beating superfast, Marco's touch did something else to me. It was a weird mixture of feeling safe but also wanting his hands on every part of my body. Very, very confusing.

"Marco, can you let go of her for like two minutes?" Croy bit out, "my wolf is having a fucking panic attack."

I frowned as Marco shook his head and muttered a curse, setting me down next to him. But then I was on another lap as Croy moved fast enough that I was across the room and in his arms in a blink. Why did everyone move so fast around here? Maybe I really was a phoenix. I was more of a glide type of girl myself.

Henry spoke, "Croy, please be careful, Maya has been through a lot. She was who we were talking about earlier."

My eyes fluttered up as the southern man made a strangled noise, "How do you know she's a phoenix? Has she shifted?"

"I died and came back to life," I murmured as a snarl broke through his throat. It should have made me jump, but instead I just continued to lean into him, completely relaxed.

Marco's growl was louder though as I shivered, curling my toes. "Croy, cut the shit. You have no idea what's been going on."

"She fucking died," he snapped out. "Clearly, there is an issue."

I began humming a soft sound thinking about how I sort of wanted pancakes right now. My humming stopped despite the room going quiet, I looked up at Henry and then Marco, "Can we make pancakes? I have never had them, but they look really good."

I really didn't like fighting.

"Don't Croy," Henry spoke harshly, "we will explain later. Maya, I will go make you-"

"I've got it," Ledger started walking over, ignoring Croy, and placing a gentle kiss on the corner of my mouth. He narrowed his eyes at the rumbling wolf before going towards the kitchen. I sighed.

"Marco? Henry? Do you mind giving me and wolfie here a moment?"

"Wolfie?" Croy asked quietly, almost upset. I just ran a hand through his hair and he muttered a curse, letting out a soft rumble leaning into it. Marco and Henry both offered me a kiss and the same glance towards my wolf before leaving. You have to understand, unlike the six flames inside of me, my magic had simply decided his wolf belonged with us. Right in the center. So here he was.

My wolf. All mine.

"Maya?" Croy asked quietly as I turned toward him and smiled. *He really was very handsome.*

"Thanks," he muttered.

"Did I say that out loud?" I grinned, blushing.

He chuckled and shook his head, "Yeah you did."

I nodded, "So wolfie, *Croy*, sorry. You seem upset, did I do something to upset you?"

His eyes flickered between my gaze and then down to my lips. I squeaked as he leaned forward and pressed his sculpted lips to mine, making a soft noise come from my throat. Mint exploded on my tongue and his hand came around the back of my head to hold me in place, shivers trailing over me skin. When he pulled back, I was bright pink and I shifted, feeling him very hard underneath me.

"That was the third kiss I've ever had," I murmured as his eyebrows went up. I smiled then and ran my hand along his chest, "you're a very good kisser though."

"Third kiss?" He rose a brow.

I shifted and he groaned. I laughed, offering a tiny smile. "Sorry Croy, I didn't want to bring it up but I'm pretty sure you find me attractive."

His eyes darkened as a low rumble came from his throat. "Yeah you could say that…"

"She means that."Anani strode in, grabbing something from the self. "Maya is new to all this, Croy. And I'm not a dick enough to get in the way of mating shit, but please bare that element in mind."

"New to all this?" He asked as I let out a soft hum and began to twist small pieces of his shiny hair. I could have sat on his lap all day long. He would totally let me to. His wolf was a sweet thing and my magic and his were cuddled up already.

"She turned eighteen yesterday, for one," Anani said bluntly as I scowled, "and she was…"

"Locked in a basement for most of my life, this past week has been very different," I noted in a cheerful tune.

Silence filled the space and then I popped my eyes up to his, "oh and I died yesterday, so you could say it's been eventful."

"18?" Croy asked grunting.

Anani finally found the item he needed and raised a brow. "Don't try acting like that bothers you Croy, you could tell damn well she's young."

"How old are you?" I asked him curiously. Anani chuckled and left the room.

He grunted, shaking his head, "been around a bit, wolves have different life spans."

"Interesting," I murmured.

"Marco," Croy called out and the man appeared nearly

instantly, standing behind me. I tilted my head up as my dragon graced me with a small smile.

"What?" He raised a brow at the man.

"You can't tell the dragon council about her."

I frowned, "Why?"

Marco smoothed a hand over the back of my neck that had everything turning warm inside of me. A shiver crawled over my skin as a flare of that dangerous boiling heat shot out, causing my breath to catch. Croy groaned and his jaw clenched.

"Marco," he snarled.

Marco chuckled, "I am not about to stop touching my mate just because she likes it and you don't."

I did. I liked it a lot.

"She hasn't hit her mating heat yet?" Croy asked frowning.

"We think it may have to do with not shifting yet," Marco said softly, "but why regarding the dragon council?"

"I worry they might try to take her," he muttered softly.

Atlas was in the room then, his brow dipping at our position and easily lifting me from him, his nose burying into my neck. I instantly felt far more relaxed and despite protests, both men let him take me into the kitchen. The twins were cooking and Henry was nowhere to be found.

Atlas sat me on the counter and braced his forearms on either side of me. I looked down at him and ran my nails through his hair.

"You're so sleepy and cuddly in the morning," he stated softly, sitting on the bar stool.

Cuddly? Like cuddling?

"What is cuddling?" I frowned.

"It's how you and I slept at night when you were living

at... home," he said softly. I knew he hated the word home in reference to that place, to be fair I did as well.

I nodded because that made sense. My lip was bit into slightly as I grinned, "What if I wanted to cuddle with you when we weren't sleeping?" I really wanted to cuddle with all of them to be honest.

"Then you better believe we would fucking cuddle." He flashed me a dangerous smile.

"Well let's," I teased.

"Pancakes," Ledger offered me a grin and laid out a plate. I immediately picked it up and Atlas grabbed syrup for me. He poured some on and then held up a bottle of whipped cream, I frowned.

"Not sure I like that," I mused.

The man squeezed some on his large finger and offered it to me. I leaned in slightly and pulled his finger into my mouth, licking it before humming and pulling away. Anani let out a curse and stormed from the room as Atlas offered me a dangerous smile.

"Sure you don't need a second taste?" He asked, his voice warm and sending chills up my spine. His eyes were more amber than gold and the flames in them made me feel like it was his dragon looking through.

"Maybe," I whispered because maybe I did. Or maybe I just liked the way he was looking at me.

Atlas' grin grew as he took some more and lifted it to my mouth, except instead he ran it along my lips as my breathing increased and chills rolled over me. My breasts were super tight and that molten explosion of heat inside of me had everything dangerously picking up.

I let my tongue dip out slightly and he leaned closer, his eyes flickering between my lips and eyes. His voice was rough, "Taste good?"

A soft hum came from my throat, "Maybe." It did.

I had to be honest I had no idea what I was doing, but man did this feel exciting.

"Can I try?" He asked.

I frowned, "Yes?"

Then I understood what he meant. A content sound came from my throat as I received my fourth freakin' kiss that had my entire body exploding with heat. My hands immediately sunk into his hair and I hesitantly slipped my tongue to entwine with his, causing a low, dangerous noise to come from his chest. A noise that had me tightening my legs around him.

"I mean I'm all for this being breakfast," Ledger purred as I jumped, pulling back slightly and blushing. The indigo eyes of my other dragon were lit with amusement and dangerous heat. "But you did want to try pancakes..."

"Oh!" I scrambled down the from the counter to sit right on Atlas's lap, his laugh making his chest shake behind me.

For the record, I didn't like the whip cream nearly as much on the pancakes as the way Atlas had us eating it.

21

SAI

I really was a fairly anti-social person.
 That came with the fighting lifestyle in the human world though. I wasn't a fan of the celebrity status or crowds of people surrounding me. I wasn't able to push it off like Marco did or enjoy it like the twins did. Well, like Anani did. It just felt manufactured for me.

What I did enjoy?

Watching Maya walk down these damn stairs as if she not only owned the place, but didn't care that four of the most important people in dragon society were watching her. Just the way Marco liked it, for the record. I swallowed hard, trying to not get caught up on how fucking perfect she looked, her dark hair pulled up and her curvy little body dressed in a pale yellow sundress that tied with a bow at the top of her neck. Other than that, she had bare feet and a big excited smile. I tried to contain my growl at every other fucking dragon male looking at her.

"Sai!" She grinned approaching me as I pulled her into my arms.

I'd always been ignored in my real family. As the

youngest of seven, I'd gotten everything second best and it hadn't bothered me. I hadn't expected to feel the level of joy that I did when Maya asked me to be her first kiss.

There were so many things I loved about Maya and one of them was her curiosity. I also loved her strength, and her ability to keep positive despite not having a reason to be. Sure, she was naive, but she was smart as a whip and able to catch onto things extremely fast. I was just crazy about the woman and that wasn't even including the mating bond.

"You look handsome," she chirped and the word sounded foreign on her tongue, like it was her first time using it out loud. But fuck if it didn't feel good to hear a compliment coming out of her lips.

"And you look beautiful," I murmured as a pink blush filled her cheeks.

The twins then approached and her grin grew. I knew she was excited to see them perform and I could practically see the fuckers' egos growing. I had zoned out for a bit, running a hand through her long ponytail, but quickly snapped to it as two very familiar women approached.

Anani's eyes went wide and I shook my head, this was going to be a mess.

"Ledger," Ainsely chimed behind him and sliding an arm around his chest, making him still. Maya seemed to freeze as Mercy also approached Anani and tossed him a grin.

"Hello," Anani stepped back slightly as Ledger removed her hand with a frown.

"Who is this?" Ainsely asked, "She's so cute!"

Maya's jaw clenched and I saw a true, nearly frightening, expression crossed her face. I rubbed her back but she stayed still, not even leaning back into it. Despite the pastel dresses and bows I had a feeling that when Maya finally came into power, she was going to be a force to be reckoned with.

"My name is Maya," she voiced, her eyes narrowing.

Mercy cooed, "So pretty, is she your little cousin or something?"

Now we were not suppose to announce we had a mate yet. Marco had said that it was important that we try to keep it low key because then the council would ask what she was, and Henry, Croy, and Marco weren't around to fix this shit. I couldn't even think about freakin' Croy right now. The point? We had no idea what to say in reference to Maya. Well, I did but you could tell the twins didn't.

"No," Ledger scowled and rounded to stand near Maya.

"So who is she?"Ainsely asked.

Maya was uncharacteristically quiet and I could almost feel her magic taking stock of the situation and evaluating the twin's response.

Anani hissed out the words, "A friend."

I wasn't sure Maya knew what Marco had instructured from us and the way her eyes flashed slightly made me think she hadn't. My mouth opened to stop her as she turned on her heel and walked toward the stone pavilion, Ledger muttering out a curse.

"Sai..." Anani spoke in a strangled tone.

"Fucking fix this," I snarled and nearly caught up to her.

Croy was there then his eyes fixated on her expression and as I rounded to where she'd stopped, I could see her eyes were dark and a bit glassy. "Maya," I mumbled, "they didn't mean..."

"What is going on?" Croy demanded as I grunted.

I think Marco and maybe Henry were the only two that were above him in rank. In the food chain you could say.

Atlas and he were about at the same level, so as much as I wanted to punch the asshole, I couldn't.

"Nothing." She sniffed slightly and frowned, "I need to go grab something..."

She slipped past again and Marco's eyes darkened as he left their table midconversation. I could see the other council members frown, but he had Maya up in his arms in a moment flat.

"Sai, what happened?" Marco demanded as Maya shook her head, trying to hold back tears. I didn't like seeing her try to control her reactions around us. I loved how authentic she was. It was refreshing as fuck.

"I'm fine." She wiggled down. "I want to go inside."

He let her as Croy followed, my mouth opening to explain. "Anani and Ledger's exes showed up and Anani, because of the direction he was given, called her 'a friend' when the girls asked."

Realization dawned on his face as he muttered a curse. "Go get the twins and tell them to fix this. I will tell the council she's our mate, but I need her down here for it."

I nodded going towards the twins and immediately both of them looked up thankfully because the two girls were practically yelling at them. I could see both of the twins getting pissed, something none of us needed. Once they lost it, it was difficult to reign them back in. I knew they were trying to maintain some level of civility. I looked at the two women. Now, I *was* higher rank than them.

"Ladies," I said sharply, "I'm going to need you to get the fuck out of here."

"What?" Mercy growled.

"I said get the fuck out," I snarled. "You upset our mate so I need you to leave."

"He said they were friends!"

"That was to keep busy bodies like you away from the situation. Now get the fuck out," I put extra emphasis on 'out' as both snarled and walked away. I narrowed my eyes at the twins but they were both already walking towards the house.

This was a fucking mess.

22
MAYA

*H*e hadn't even said anything mean.
    He really hadn't. *Friend* was a good term, but the thing inside me had hated that. Hated that he hadn't said 'mate' because it felt like it would have forced the women back and made it clear that they weren't allowed to touch them. God, were they beautiful though. It was so frustrating. I was so tiny compared to them and they were dressed in these snake skin like dresses that I didn't even like, but they just seemed older.

Was that what the twins liked?

I wasn't positive I would feel comfortable wearing that.

My eyes blinked with tears as I sat on the bed in my room and Croy appeared looking concerned. Immediately, he was crouched down in front of me and I didn't hide the tears on my face. I didn't understand an article I'd read about hiding your emotions. How did you hide them? They existed so you had to show them. Right?

I may have felt silly being upset, but I was still very much that. Upset.

"Sugar." His accent thick and making me all warm and nervous. "I know you're upset, I don't think they meant it..."

"I know," I whispered cupping his jaw, "I know they didn't. I'd heard Marco talking to all of you about keeping it away from the council because they could act weird about what I am. I just really didn't like those girls."

"That's because they are bitches," Croy muttered.

"Croy," I laughed softly. "I didn't go that far."

"Of course you didn't Sugar, because you're sweet."

"You say that like it's a bad thing, is it?" I asked curiously, loving the way his eyes lit up.

"No, I think it's perfect," Croy flashed a smile. Have you ever met someone and despite not knowing them that well, felt a connection? Not even supernatural completely. I just felt good around Croy. He settled something in me. It was like, now that I had the seven of them, I felt complete.

A knock on the door had both of us looking up as a dangerous sound left his chest. You know, I was starting to think the men I was around were a tad dangerous. It probably didn't make a lot of sense to be comfortable around Croy, but he was mine. He was my wolf.

"Just call me if you need anything," Croy mumbled, kissing my forehead and leaving me with the twins.

"Firefly," Ledger whispered.

"Hey," I mumbled softly.

I wish I'd felt as confident as I had with Becky Ash. But there was a difference. Henry had told me he didn't feel anything towards her. The twins hadn't.

"Peanut." Anani crouched down so they were eye level with my position at the end of the bed.

"I'm sorry," I whispered, "I shouldn't have run away like that."

"No, Maya," Anani moved to the bed so I was now

between the twins in the center of the cushioned pillow. "That was on us, we could have found a different way to handle it."

"Or just told them the truth," Ledger grunted. "Marco be damned."

My lip twitched at that because Marco would totally hate it. I sighed and I spoke the honest truth. "I didn't want to assume how you felt about all this. Croy, Marco, Atlas, and Sai have made it," I blushed, "pretty freakin' clear they like me. I think Henry did as well, but I never really talked to you two about it, so I didn't know if maybe you did like them."

Anani got a pained look on his face, "First of all, Maya, of course we fucking like you."

"Probably more than that," Ledger muttered, looking stressed, "and we aren't going to lie to you, Firefly, we did date them for like less than a month."

"About six months ago," Anani finished, "but they only wanted to be with us because of our band. It was one of the final straws on why we took a step back."

I swallowed and nodded, "That makes sense."

"Why do you think we don't like you like that?" Ledger frowned.

I nibbled my lip and spoke quietly after a slight hesitation, "Well, you haven't kissed me."

See? That was honest.

A low vibrating sound came from Ledger's throat as an odd shift took over the air, my eyes flirting between the two of them. Anani grasped my jaw as a small, almost dark smile took over his face. "So all we need to do is kiss you to convince you?"

I blushed and nodded slowly because I felt like that was a good measure. Right?

"I mean, brother," Ledger drawled, "we can't have her doubting us."

Then Anani's lips pressed to mine and everything inside of my chest lit up. I moaned into it slightly as he let out a low growl and slipped his tongue into my mouth. My body arched forward as another pair of hands ran up my waist and spine in a rhythmic pattern that had my heart beating fast. I pulled away, practically out of breath as Anani's crystal eyes darkened.

A small, almost needy sound came out of me as Ledger wrapped a hand around my throat and tipped it back so he was almost kissing me upside down. My center tightened and when Anani's hands traveled up my waist, I realized what I needed. The boiling under my skin jumped as both men groaned and I grasped Anani's hands to bring them to my tight breasts. It was almost painful, the feeling under my skin, like I was boiling from the inside out.

He muttered a curse, but began to do exactly what I needed. When my dress slipped down to my waist as Ledger untied it, I pulled back from the kiss only momentarily.

"You sure you're okay with this, Peanut ?" Anani asked softly.

I nodded as my eyes fluttered and I let out a small moan, his mouth closing over my nipple as Ledger's lips began to trail down my neck. His hard length was pressed right against my butt and I rocked back as his large hands crawled around the front of me and slipped beneath the pooled material of dress around my waist. When his fingers met my center, I whimpered as Anani's teeth bit down lightly on my other nipple.

"Fuck, you are so wet," Ledger groaned, his fingers slipping right into me, causing me to cry out and drop my head back onto his shoulder. His pace was a bit faster than Marco's and it had me practically shaking with need. I barely noticed as Anani ripped the material of silky panties on either side and pulled the dress over my head.

All I could feel was the two sets of hands on me and both of their lips. One at my neck and the other trailing down the center of my body as I leaned into Ledger. My eyes flung open as Anani's tongue met my clit. And yes, I knew what that was. I wasn't that naive. Well, I had been but after what Marco had made me feel? I needed to know more.

Apparently, and this is going to kill you, what happened to me was called 'cumming' and yes, it was spelled that way and everything. Crazy.

"Oh shit," I breathed out as Ledger chuckled but continued to pump his fingers in and out of me, now from behind, as Anani's tongue circled my clit again and again. My eyes began to flutter and it was maybe moments before I let out a gasp, my hands sinking into Anani's hair, as the feeling I was looking for reached a near peak.

When his teeth grazed that center bundle of nerves, I let out a small cry and my center tightened right around Ledger's fingers, everything exploding out. I shattered and a shiver rolled over me, making me feel nearly dizzy with relief and my eyes became hooded. *Oh thank god.*

"Oh wow," I sighed as Anani's lips met mine and a different taste, my taste, pressed between us. A feeling of ownership over him filled me and I wanted everyone to know that he was mine. It was possessive. I felt possessive over him.

Ledger turned me so we could kiss and I ran my hands through his orange tipped hair.

"Convinced we like you?" Anani nibbled my ear as I let out an authentic laugh.

"Even I'm fucking convinced," Henry's voice sounded as all three of us snapped our heads over and a smile took over my face. Henry.

"Yes," I whispered. Henry approached me and I couldn't even feel shy about my bare body.

Henry, despite sometimes coming off as shy, had this power to him I couldn't describe. He tilted my head back slightly and pressed a gentle kiss to my lips that had me shivering. Then he tugged on my bottom lip, hard enough that it bled. His tongue rolling over the injury to soothe it before pulling back. I felt nearly dizzy at his touch.

"Marco needs you downstairs and you two have a show to do, plans have changed. Maya is our mate and I don't give a fuck who knows."

I grinned as he walked out and Anani chuckled, shaking his head. Ledger pulled my dress on over my head and none of us made mention of my lack of panties. I hoped up and brushed my fingers through my hair. Ledger spoke, "Henry is such a control freak, I can't imagine what it's going to be like when he breaks one day."

"Breaks?" I raised a brow.

Anani winked, "yeah, I think that's exactly what you're gonna do to him, Peanut , break him."

Now that sounded a bit exciting the way they were talking about it.

Once downstairs, Marco met me by the back door and he inhaled, his eyes darkening before looking at the twins. "Really?"

"Does she look unhappy to you?" Ledger raised a brow and they were out the door. I may have smiled watching them walk away. Did I mention they had sort of cute butts? Was that a thing?

"Are you okay, honey?" Marco asked softly as I tilted my chin up grinning.

"Yeah I am."

He nodded, "good, come on then. I want you to meet the council."

I didn't have time to be nervous before Marco had led me to the table from the other night and sat me on his knee, my smile serene as he ran a hand up and down my bare back.

"Who is this Marco?" A dark almost clinical voice asked. I moved my gaze from his to a pair of dark eyes from across the table. The man sitting there was handsome, but there was a distinct coldness to him that made me a bit uncomfortable.

"This is my flight's mate, Maya," he responded cooly as Henry sat down. I wondered where Atlas was briefly.

"Your mate?" Another man responded sharply. This man had pale blonde hair and orange colored skin which was very unique looking.

"So I guess no more playtime then?" A female voice asked in a husky tone. I froze because I somehow knew exactly what she was insinuating. Instead of getting worked up, I simply leaned into Marco and met her pale gray eyes with a small smile. I didn't even realize Marco was growling until Henry spoke.

"Councilwoman Anna," Henry clipped, "you know as well as everyone here, Marco hasn't touched you. Ever. If you're going to be problematic, I would suggest you remember this is our private property and you don't need to be here."

Another man chuckled as she snarled and stood up,

walking off. Now her? I may consider her a bitch. I knew Marco, even from the short time, and while their past was a bit of a mystery to me. I trusted him. With everything.

"I'm sorry about that, Sweetheart," he murmured.

"Could have been worse," Henry noted.

"What type of shifter are you?" The cold man asked.

I sat up and looked to Marco, his hand smoothing over my neck in a possessive way. His eyes warmed and he nodded. "I'm a phoenix."

Someone dropped the fork they were using.

"Prove it," the man with bright hair and orange skin snarled.

"I died Friday morning and now I'm here," I spoke softly. "I don't need to prove any more to you. If you don't want to believe me, that is your own prerogative."

The smiling, relaxed man spoke, "I'm going to go get a drink, good choice boys."

His carmel hair shifted in the wind and for an older man, he really was handsome. He tossed me a wink and walked off. That left us with *orangey* and *meanie*.

"You understand how rare that is?" The cold man snapped. "If she is, then she needs to be introduced to other flights..."

"Absolutely fucking not," Marco growled in a savage snarl, his arms tightening around me. "Is that understood Councilman? My mate is not going anywhere fucking near another flight."

"Why would I want to visit other flights?" I asked curiously as Henry watched me with amusement and hooded eyes. I'm not sure what I was doing that was so amusing.

"You have to see if they are truly your mates," the orange skinned man spoke.

"Not necessary, I know they are," I softly stated with a

grin. "Plus Marco already bit me and I bit him. So he's mine."

Now I was feeling possessive.

"You marked her?!" The cold one snarled.

"I marked him first," I stated in a relaxed tone, "also do you mind lowering your voice? We have other guests."

The cold one narrowed his eyes at me and stood up, stalking off. Hmm. My friendship skills may be lacking. Henry chuckled and kissed my hand as Marco nibbled on my neck slightly as orangey spoke.

"You know she still has to be formally introduced to all the ruling flights because you're a councilman." He smirked. "Even as a formality."

"I have no issue with them meeting her after she is marked by my flight," Marco hissed.

Croy sat down where carmel hair had been and smiled at me. Then his face turned dark as he looked at the man, "Why does my mate look upset, Larry?"

Ew. That name. So we had Larry and Anna. Had those names down.

Larry's eyes widened, "she's mated to a wolf as well? You can't do that, if she truly is a phoenix..."

"Leave," Henry bit out, "get out of here, now." Croy was producing an actual growl and my center warmed at his defense over us.

"This isn't over," Larry snarled. "Lucas may be proud of your antics, but Edmund agrees with me. You still have to answer the council, Marco, despite being on it."

Then he was gone. Wow, Marco did hold a lot of power.

"I don't think they like me," I noted amused.

"Good," Marco grumbled, "fucking assholes."

"You swear a lot," I grinned as the man's ears turned pink and he narrowed his eyes at me.

Before he could respond, my head snapped up as the music began. I was up and out of my seat, with Croy following.

Now, I had never been to a performance, but I knew what looked cool. They looked cool. Ledger was standing back, holding a guitar along with three other people on stage I didn't know. Anani stood right at the microphone and winked at me.

He said a tiny introduction that had the crowd cheering, I pushed towards the center of the stage. There were a lot of people here. I hadn't realized. Croy lifted me up and sat me on his right shoulder so that I could keep my legs crossed and his hands kept me securely fixed.

Then the twins made my night.

"This entire show is for our beautiful little mate, Maya," Anani's voice was smooth and I smiled as people turned back to see me. I grinned as their music started up and the minute Anani started singing and Ledger started playing, I knew I was in for something special.

WHEN I WOKE up the next morning, I was in bed with Marco and Henry. I knew I'd started out with the twins, but I'd woken up in the middle of the night and crawled into bed with them. Now Marco had his chest against my back and head buried in my neck where Henry had his arms looped around my waist and his head resting on my chest. I hummed softly and stretched feeling both of them shift awake. I shivered as both of them hardened against me.

"Morning," Marco drawled his teeth biting down softly and causing me to shiver.

Henry looked up at me from where his lips rested on my neck, "You smell so damn sweet, Maya."

I was about to say something, but the door swung open and a very sleepy Croy spoke. "You need to get down here, now. Security is barely holding back the media at the gates."

"The fuck?" Henry muttered and stood up. I crawled to the end of the bed as Croy lifted me up and we all went to stand by the windows.

Oh wow.

"Why?" I whispered.

"You," Marco muttered.

"Me?" I whispered. "They weren't this bad when we first got here."

"Apparently, it got out that the police are looking for you back in Washington," Croy mumbled.

"What?" Henry snapped out.

Croy walked over the large television as I was put down. My feet were a bit chilled on the cool surface, but I watched as the surface lit up with a network called CNN.

My picture, between ones of Atlas and Marco, popped up.

"Police have not disclosed yet if this is a case of attempting to flee or if the socialites didn't consider that they would be associated with the death of Jed Mara and Tina Lucas."

"It is important to note that the woman, Maya, is a high school student at..."

I stopped listening. Henry shook his head, "We disposed of the bodies and everything."

"What bodies?" Croy bit out.

"I was locked in a church basement and only arrived here about a week ago. My mother, Tina, and her boyfriend, Jed, beat me until I died. The boys showed up and killed them, I was reborn and now we are here," I explained simply.

"They are saying they got the information from one of the co-owners of the rental dwelling."

"So one of his lackeys," Marco snarled.

Croy was still staring at me with really wide eyes. I squeezed his hand and he simply muttered a curse before pulling me close and burying his nose in my hair. They were always doing that. I hoped my hair smelled good.

"We need to get back," I murmured.

Marco was on the phone talking to someone as Henry called for Atlas. The man showed up looking aggravated, but pressed a kiss to my forehead before they started to talk about things I wasn't well versed in. Croy even joined in. I shook my head and decided to do something in the meantime.

I turned to go towards my room, both twins still sleeping, and got into the shower. I hummed softly, washing off all the sand and anything else from last night before wrapping a robe securely around myself. I'd never used hair product before and now that I did, I wasn't positive how I hadn't before. My long brown hair hung to my waist and I rubbed this vanilla lip gloss on before walking to my closet and picking out a comfortable outfit.

A pair of black high waisted pants and a cropped sweater in a forest green. I paired it with these shoes called 'ballet flats' and grabbed my purse. I wasn't positive where my bag was to pack up, but I would probably just leave some of the stuff here. I hoped we came back.

This has oddly been exactly what I needed.

"Where are you going?" Marco asked as I headed downstairs passing him.

"I was going to ask them to leave us alone," I stated.

Henry offered me a wide eyed look before Marco grinned. "Bad idea honey, trust me. They are vicious animals."

"Marco," I smirked, "you're a dragon. They can't be much more vicious."

He shook his head, "come on, through the garage, we are going to head out as it is."

"But the twins..."

"Are ready to go," Ledger yawned.

I followed after them into the garage and Croy stopped, "I have an idea."

Marco sighed, "I already know what you're going to say."

"What?" I perked up.

Marco cupped my jaw and searched my eyes, "They are going to expect you to be in this car, so I want you to go in Croy's to the airport, is that okay?"

"Sure," I grinned, "Croy is cool."

"Kitten," Sai scowled, "you literally have never used that word before and now you are using it on Croy."

"Because I am cool," Croy winked.

Marco looked at Croy, "If she is at all injured, I fucking mean even a papercut..."

"Marco," Croy growled slightly. "She's perfectly fine. I have no paper in my car and on top of that, I haven't stayed alive as long as I have by being reckless.

Both twins offered me a searing kiss as Marco pressed one on my temple. Atlas approached and brushed his nose against mine, "Stay safe, call me if you have any issues."

I nodded, not really ever checking for my phone, but somehow knowing it was in my purse.

Sai approached, grabbing my hips and leaning forward, tugging on mine so he could invade my mouth, which had me shivering. Henry muttered a curse before pulling me into a hug, kissing my neck and speaking quietly, "You and I are having alone time later."

"Oh, why?" I asked.

Croy chuckled, shaking his head, coming up behind me, looking at Henry over my shoulder. "Yes, Henry. Why?"

Henry nipped at my skin and caused my breathing to heighten. Croy 'tsked' and pulled me over to his impressive sleek little car, opening the door for me and making sure I was buckled. Instantly, I began playing with buttons and the low purr was overrun by music. I smiled at the guitar that reminded me so much of Ledger.

"You like the Led Zeppelin?" Croy chuckled sliding in effortlessly.

"Sure?" I raised a brow.

He tilted his head looking over me with interest and pulled out of the garage. Instantly the gates opened as security kept the camera people and trucks from blocking our path. I think it worked because everyone was craning their head to see the black SUV behind us about 20 feet, so our sleek car slid past with ease and I finally sat up fully once we were driving down the street.

"If the cops are looking for me, why haven't they showed up?" I asked quietly.

"They already contacted Marco, the human enforcement are causing issues with the media but the supernatural jurisdiction in Washington has it mostly handled. Even the FBI office around there is supe run. We just need to get you back there. You said those two tried to kill you?"

"They did kill me," I murmured.

He looked over at me and frowned. "Sugar, I don't understand how I didn't know you were out there."

"Probably because I wasn't," I sighed. "I was locked in a basement until about 12 days ago."

He frowned and then chuckled, "That would explain the dream I had."

"What dream?"

He tilted his head, "Just about a woman, and now I'm thinking it was about you. Happened around that time frame. I wonder what wards they had on the church you were in."

"Wards?"

"Yes, to keep you in no doubt," he sighed. "Humans, after all this time, are as primitive and scared as before."

"How old are you Croy?" I asked sincerely.

His eyes flash dark, "You sure you want to know that, Maya?"

I grinned at how my name sounded on his lips, "Yeah, I do."

"Two hundred twenty-four," he stated softly.

"Holy crap," I mumbled as his eyes traced the curiosity in my face and he relaxed slightly. "That is really cool."

"It's something," he mumbled.

"No really," I grasped his hand on the center console, "it is really neat." It was! I bet he had a lot of interesting things that had happened to him. Honestly, I was taking advantage of everyone else's life experiences to make up for my lack of them.

He smiled and kissed my hand before continuing to drive, my body content and relaxed.

It was only as we neared the airport that I worried about how we were going to get onto the plane. There were people everywhere.

23

CROY

My wolf rumbled aggressively as we neared the airport and security let us through the gate. I hated this. I hated how many people there were and I hated how Maya had to see humanity like this. She was clearly so new to this world, something I found far more attractive than I would have expected.

Then again, I thought I'd nearly had a heart attack when she stepped down those stairs.

Have you ever had a moment where things seem to slow? Like truly nearly stop. In the over two centuries I'd been on this plane, I'd never in my life had a moment like that. When her soft voice had echoed through the space every part of me had collided towards her to the symphony of 'mate.' She was my mate. Mine.

Rationally, I knew she wasn't only mine, but I wasn't 100% positive that mattered right now. My hand closed over her thigh as we moved through the gates and a small pulsating moment of pride hit me because I could tell my touch affected her. Her breathing quickened and legs shifted, making me want to stop the car and pull her over the center console.

I couldn't though.

I knew she wasn't ready for that, no matter how badly I wanted to sink right into her.

It was odd seeing this group of men so damn possessive over someone. Not only that, but it was like she'd softened the entire space. Not to say they were cruel or mean before, but to people outside of their group? They weren't exactly fantastic. I mean, Marco was well known enough the human crime syndicates stayed the fuck away from his territories.

I was distracted enough by my thoughts that when a figure darted out in front of my car, I threw on the breaks and Maya squeaked. My lips pressed together as the paparazzi snapped photos of the two of us, airport security moving their slow, lazy asses over to get him. Maya watched with confusion and interest before I tried to distract her.

"Sugar?" I asked quietly.

"Yes?" She turned toward me slightly as I drove closer to the plane. I hadn't left LA in forever and leaving now seemed like no big deal because the much bigger deal was her.

"What's your favorite color?" I asked curiously as I parked my car. Looking around, I saw we'd passed tighter security so I got out and rounded it, so she could answer me. I helped her out and she tossed me a smile, straightening her purse.

"Pink," she chimed. "Oh, and glitter!"

Of course it was. I never thought someone so feminine would appeal to me considering my life-style but I had to admit, the shit just made me want to wrap her up forever. We walked up the plane steps right as the other SUV made it in and I followed her back to a cushioned seat. She yawned and stretched her body like a sated kitten.

"I'm glad you are coming with us," she whispered.

I smiled as she tucked her head against my chest and fell asleep. I was glad that made her happy because I wasn't sure I could leave at this point.

The one thing I was thankful for? Despite their frustration, they understood better than anyone to not try to stop mated situations. So here I was and no one was trying to stop this. I would lose my shit if they did and it helped that Maya said she wanted me here.

As everyone loaded onto the plane, I shared a look with Henry because, for the first time in nearly two centuries, I was feeling something so strong I could barely describe it.

24

MAYA

"You just flew to freakin' LA for the weekend?" Jordan plopped down next to me at lunch.

Henry made a frustrated noise but I smiled at my red haired friend.

"We did," I nodded, "I didn't get any pictures."

"Oh honey," she grinned, "you didn't need to."

I raised my brows as she slid her phone towards me on an app called 'Snapchat' and the newsfeed seemed to feature little stories. My brows went up at the headline 'Moretti's Shared Mistress.' I snorted and Jordan nodded, amused.

"Well, I sort of like those photos," I pointed out even though they were clearly made to make me look bad.

"I do as well," she noted and then crossed her arms on the table top looking at me. "So what are you doing after school today?"

"I'm working," I grin, really excited.

She snorts and looks at the three men at the table, all offering grunts I didn't understand. "Where at?"

"Clara's Crafts."

"No shit?" She grins. "That's my grandma's shop."

"Really?" I smiled, "I love that."

"I work Tuesday through Thursday, so we will have joint shifts," she adds.

I went to respond when a shadow shifted over us. I squeaked as Henry's arm wrapped around me tight and a growl came from his mouth. Even Jordan stilled as I looked up at... Seth, was it?

"Maya," Seth grinned, "Jordan."

"Seth," Jordan warned, "you know this is a terrible idea."

He grinned and shrugged, "Can't live without asking."

"Asking what?" I frowned. Malloy was sitting quietly and watching Seth with a frustrated expression I didn't fully understand.

Seth tilted his head and spoke, "Would you like to go on a date, Maya?"

"What?"

Ledger stood up and snarled, "Get the fuck out of here, Seth."

"Not until I get her answer."

I frowned. Date? I didn't really know what a date was fully. Wasn't it when a couple went out together? But I had never gone on a date with my mates. Malloy seemed affected by his words because my friend, yes actual friend, got up without a word. Seth's cheerfulness seemed to fade as he watched him walk away. What was I not understanding here?

"What's a date?" I voiced as Anani muttered a curse and Seth barked out a laugh.

Henry was there then, in his face, gripping his shirt. "I'd highly suggest you get the fuck out of here."

Seth tossed me a wink and threw up his hands. "If you

ever want to be treated right, let me know Maya. Bye, Jordan."

My friend sighed and Henry sat back down next to me. Jordan stood and squeezed my shoulder looking over the three of them. "I would highly suggest you show her what a date is, boys. You're making it far too easy for someone else to sweep in."

"We've been busy," Ledger muttered.

Jordan was gone, following after Malloy and Seth, and I quirked a brow, "What is a date? It's for couples, right? But we have never gone on any."

"We clearly need to change that," Henry stated softly.

"Why do all of you look upset?"

"Did you want to go on that date with Seth?" Anani asked seriously as I frowned.

"If you're asking if I like him how I like you, of course I don't," I reasoned, "but I think he is nice. He's never done anything to hurt me and, except for today, hasn't caused problems."

"Oh, he's gonna be a fucking problem," Ledger muttered.

I opened my mouth, "I really don't think so, Malloy and him…"

It really wasn't our day because Lorn interrupted my thoughts. This one actually made me angry. I frowned as he narrowed his eyes at the boys before tossing me a sick smile.

"I heard you're a fugitive, killed mommy and daddy," he snarled.

"Does your father know you're looking through his files?" Henry snapped.

Lorn put his hands up. "Just saw it on the news."

I believed that. As predicted, when we'd gotten home, the police had been there, waiting.

"Now Maya, we need to know exactly what happened." It was one of the shifter cops.

Marco had told me to tell them the truth while he talked to the human ones outside.

So I told them. I told them everything from the moment I'd left the church until now. I trusted that I could because these were the same two men who kept me safe and watched outside my trailer. I had learned that one was named Richard and the other Steven. Both had little kids under the age of ten and I could see how much my story upset them.

They'd believed me though, and once they had the statement, they gathered the human cops, both leering at me. Something that Atlas snapped at them about before they left. Leaving me feeling exhausted and like memory lane was becoming my reality for the night.

Now I sat here, hearing about how the human version is spreading across the media. How I had run away because of their abuse but hadn't seen them since Tuesday night after the police incident. How they were drug users and how Jed had a record. Connecting the evidence. So you have to imagine that Lorn was making me a tad upset.

"Listen Lorn," I snapped, feeling frustrated, "you need to leave."

He sneered, "Yeah, Maya? Weird how you have so much confidence now, with six dragons backing you up."

I stood and stepped closer to him feeling frustration and anger simmer under the surface. His eyes widened as I spoke carefully, "You're a jerk, Lorn. I don't know what your problem is, but you need to leave now."

"Or what?" He bit out.

I lifted a finger and pressed it into his shirt, right as the man's shirt sizzled like someone had pressed a cigarette into it. He jumped back and I watched him scoff but pale.

"Whatever," he muttered with a snarl walking away.

"I don't use the word annoying very often," I pointed out, "but the man's annoying."

"Understatement, Peanut," Anani pointed out. Henry was looking at my finger in slight shock and Ledger had this big goofy grin on his lips.

The lunch room doors opened and it was like everyone had decided to be a problem today. A very human officer walked in and he immediately started walking towards us, my bravado fading. Lorn was scary, but he was starting to frustrate me. This guy had a gun and everything, it made me nervous.

"Maya?" An officer confirmed as everyone looked at us.

"You have absolutely no right to be here," Henry pointed out his chest rumbling.

"I do, I have permission from the principal," he stated and looked back at me. I heard Ledger get on the phone immediately and I swallowed as the man sat down across from me. His eyes were cruel and sharp.

"What do you need?" I asked quietly.

"I need to know what happened. You understand why it is hard for me to believe you had no idea your parents were dead until yesterday, right?"

"This is out of line," Henry snapped. "Maya, you don't need to say a fucking word."

Anani's arms closed around me.

I swallowed, "Jed wasn't my father."

His eyes lit up, "So you could say there is some resentment there?"

"Don't," Henry whispered softly. I inhaled and leaned back into Henry as Anani ran a hand through my hair. My lips tilted as I heard someone shouting in the hall.

Marco.

"This is fucking ridiculous," he roared out as the principal scattered after him, "I don't even want to fucking explain to you the shit you're in. You can expect to hear from my lawyer in the next hour. Officer Truce, get the fuck away from her, now."

Every single supernatural shifter froze in response to his voice and humans looked around concerned. Officer Truce, presumily, jumped and I grinned.

"Marco," I stood and he rounded the table and leaned down to kiss my forehead.

He spoke roughly, "I'll be home in a bit, honey. Henry?"

"Got it," Henry snarled at the officer and grabbed my waist gently. Both twins nodded a goodbye and I sighed, sort of missing them already. I tucked myself closer to Henry who was vibrating with a very dangerous energy.

Once he had helped me into my dark jacket and we left the school building, his voice went rough. "That was a bunch of bullshit."

"Henry..."

"No, Maya. I have no idea who the fuck he thinks he is..."

We were closer to the car as he placed me into the seat and I spoke, "Henry..."

The car door closed and he was still mumbling walking around the front of the dark car. I was sort of excited to get home and see Croy. He had taken the guest bedroom and I wondered where Atlas and Sai were as well. I went to ask, but Henry was still muttering. I sighed.

"Henry!" I called out as he froze and snapped his head to the side.

I reached forward and grabbed his shirt gently leaning over the console, slamming my lips to his. Surprised for only a moment, Henry let out a smooth hum before he slid a hand into my hair. I could feel his frantic heartbeat slowing and I pulled back as he offered me a smoldering look.

"That was naughty of you, Maya," he whispered softly, looking down at my lips before letting out a dangerous, frustrated sound. He threw the car into drive and in some ways I felt like I had instigated something more dangerous. I shivered as he drove fast and in silence, the melodic beat of something playing on the radio. Dangerous and smooth, causing the atmosphere to peak into a heated tone.

When he pulled up to the house, I realized there were no other cars here and before I could ask Henry spoke, "Croy is handling some business and the other two are at Marco's office handling something."

Oh.

Then the car was off and I watched as he strode around and those metallic dark eyes heated. He pulled me from the car and lifted me, my legs wrapped around him naturally and his large hands slipped under my thighs. I was already trembling with excitement and he pushed through the front door with ease, pressing me into the inside foyer wall.

"Henry!" I gasped as his lips slammed onto mine.

"Maya," he groaned and a deep rumble had me tightening my legs around him, his warm tongue pressing into my mouth.

His kiss was heated and smooth. His hands roaming my body like he already had my number. Had my entire self. I slipped my hands through his thick blonde hair and he pulled back slightly, his eyes flicking to the family room.

"Maybe you should go upstairs, Sweetie. I'm not exactly in control of myself right now."

I nibbled my lip, "I don't mind. I don't mind at all." *That was the honest truth.*

He muttered a curse and before I knew it, his lips were

back on mine. Devouring me. I could feel his dragon pushing out and when my butt hit the couch, I watched his eyes darken into nearly black. His knees hit the floor in front of me, those rough hands pushing up my school skirt as he pulled me forward. I squeaked and he pressed his lips to the inside of my knee gently before speaking roughly.

"Tell me to stop, Sweetie," he whispered quietly.

"I would, if I wanted you to," I whispered softly, my throat a near whimper.

His snarl was dark and dangerous, as he tugged my shirt forward and melded our lips together. I squeaked as his hands ripped my school polo down the center with ease. Jesus Christ. I moaned as his lips pressed against my skin, as his teeth pulled at the lace covering my tight breasts and hard nipples. My center was growing wetter and hotter every moment as he pulled on my nipple with his teeth and then lapped at it with his tongue.

"Henry," I cried out, "please."

"Please what?" He snarled quietly.

My thighs began to shake and my skirt was pushed up above my waist with ease. Then his mouth began to trail the inside of my thighs and then he kissed over my lace covered center, inhaling.

"Fuck, you smell so damn good," He groaned and then a snap had my panties ripping. *Oh, come on. I was going to have none left at the rate these men were ripping them.*

I whimpered as his tongue met my center. Oh, Holy Christ. My hands pulled at his hair as he began to devour me with ease, his hot mouth began to suck, nibble, and feast on my wet center.

"I could stay between your fucking legs for centuries," he growled, the vibration causing me to shake as he slipped a finger inside of me. My hips arched forward and I gripped the leather seat, wanting to touch him more. I pulled at his shirt.

"Off," I demanded softly, my voice coming out far different than expected.

He pulled away to tug it off and my eyes went wide. I had known Henry was muscular, but holy crap, his entire chest was covered in muscles with black markings. My legs were spread further as he went back to devouring me and I arched back, my head falling against the leather couch behind me. I cried out as he sucked on my clit and I nearly shot off the couch.

"Henry!" I gasped.

"Oh shit, Baby," he drawled, looking nearly frenzied, "keep saying my name."

I didn't think it was an option, I started chanting it. Then he really did it. He hummed against my clit and slipped another finger in. I cried out and came on his fingers, hard. My entire center squeezed and black stars flickered before my eyes.

Henry's teeth bit down right on the inside of my thigh and I screamed out, our bond pulsating as he snapped his eyes up with a snarl. He looked completely unhinged. His eyes black and lips stained blood red. I leaned forward and met his lips, tasting my blood. My body hit right into him and he fell back onto the floor as I crawled up his body.

"I want to taste you also," I murmured against his lips.

He growled and I followed his lead, kissing down his impressive chest, curiously running my hands and lips over every muscular dip. I had never felt so free as I did in that moment. I reached his dress pants belt, and undid it while popping open the button.

"What do I do?" I asked softly with excitement.

"Maya, Baby, you don't have to..."

"I want to," I licked my lips, tasting blood as he easily shrugged down his pants and I stared at his hardening member. I immediately ran my hand over it, despite it being covered by boxers. My fingers slipped under the band and I pulled it down to reveal... oh wow.

Now, I had never seen one this close up. I immediately took him in my hand and squeezed slightly, his growl vibrating the air around us. It was so hard and rigid yet smooth. As I continued to rub my hand up and down his hardening length, my mark throbbed. That gave me an idea. I quickly leaned down and bit his thigh where he had bitten me. He hissed out a breath as the bond snapped fully into place and his dragon produced a low dangerous sound. As the blood stopped dripping from his would, I looked up and noticed there was moisture on the end. I leaned forward to run my tongue around the tip, tasting the saltiness that exploded in my mouth.

Henry practically shot off the floor.

"Holy shit, Maya," he snarled.

"Was that wrong?" I raised a brow.

"Shit no," he growled. "Come bring that pretty mouth over here."

I did and he was on his forearms braced looking at me. He tugged on my lip gently and and then spoke, "I want you to take me into that gorgeous mouth and throat."

Immediately, I leaned down and took his hard member into my mouth. I shivered at how full my mouth felt and his hands sunk into my hair, tightening gently and forcing himself further down my throat. Saltiness exploded and his rumble had me enthusiastically bobbing my head up and down. Honestly, the noises he made were making me all that much more excited.

"Your mouth is so fucking perfect," he snarled, tightening his grip.

"Where do you want me to cum?" He asked after a groan.

What are my options?

"Do you want me to cum in your little mouth?" His voice thick with heat. I nodded and then choked on his length as he produced a low rumble. I had no idea how long he used my mouth, but I was somehow more wet and turned on than before.

His movements came faster and I shivered, my legs tightening as he grew larger in my mouth. Then, out of nowhere, he roared out my name and exploded in my mouth. Oh shit. I swallowed down an explosion of salty cum and sucked on him further as his hands tightened painfully. My legs tightened together as a small orgasm rocked through me. I pulled back finally and looked up at him.

"What the heck was that?" I raised my brows, "I didn't expect to have to swallow anything."

Henry looked at me for a heated second before barking out a laugh and laying back. "Oh Christ. Maya, I think I'm falling in love with you." *Wait, I'd been completely serious about that.*

I blushed crawling up his body so that I could rest my cheek on his chest. I decided I'd ask more about him cuming later. "What does love feel like?" That was an honest question because I'd never experienced it, so how could I recognize it?

Henry, his chuckling slowing, runs a hand through my hair. "I imagine it feels like this, little mate."

His lips met mine before he tugged up his pants and I fixed my bra and skirt for some semblance of looking normal, *good thing too*. The door opened as I blushed and Henry just tucked me closer to him, both of us still laying out against the couch on the rug covered floor.

"Henry? Maya?" Marco called out coming into the house as I turned bright red.

"In here," Henry goaded.

Then Marco turned the corner, freezing while looking at both of us. It was a silent moment as I grinned, just slightly. Then Marco barked out a laugh and shook his head. "Henry, I was gone for one fucking hour."

"A full hour?" I raised my brows looking at Henry.

He offered me a cocky smirk, "Time flies when you're having fun."

"What happened with the police officer?" I asked suddenly as Henry growled. I guess that's what had gotten him all worked up. Interesting...

Marco started talking and my eyes began to flutter closed because it sounded like he had handled everything. I curled into Henry and before I knew it, I was falling asleep. My legs pressed together as his mark pulsated, Henry tugging on my ear.

Sleepiness overtook me, surrounded by my two mates.

25

LEDGER

"How is her job not done yet?" Anani groaned. I could see her through the window, both of us sitting in the car as rain poured down. Inside of the small craft shop, our little mate was gracing the area with her charm. She had these cute white jean overalls on, with a bright shirt and these little gym shoes. It should have been goofy looking but somehow she looked stunning with brown waves cascading around her face gently. I could see paint splattering her skin as she worked with a group of little kids.

"Seeing her with kids is killing me," I muttered.

"Right?" Anani growled, "I could just fucking imagine her dancing around our kitchen one day with our kids."

"Dude," I muttered, "stop."

"You know we haven't had a boring day since Maya came into our life," Anani mused trying to be light hearted about the recent shit show. "You think it will always be like this?"

I shrugged, "Maybe?"

Both of us froze as a large dark truck pulled up next to us, the side front door painted with a large cross. My eyes narrowed on the glass, seeing the reflection of it being a Louisiana license plate. I shared a look with my brother and both of us were out immediately, my eyes narrowing on the driver's seat.

Maya looked up as the two of us entered into the shop. Jordan's grandma looked up at us and it was odd that she was human, but apparently she wasn't her biological grandma. Something about her mother's stepmom.

"Hey guys," Maya grinned. "You're here early."

"Just missed you," Anani stated as I kissed her forehead.

"Is that your husband?" A little girl chirped, "my mom just got a new husband."

"Oh wow," I muttered and then the door chime rang out from someone entering.

Maya's head snapped over there and immediately the color drained from her face and her eyes darkened. I frowned and turned to find a tall, pale man standing in the doorway, dressed in all black with a dark hat.

"Can we help you?" Clara asked, looking defensive because of Maya's reaction.

"Maya?" The man spoke his voice thick and angry. I watched as he took off his hat and Maya's eyes went massive, her breathing quickening.

"Pastor Malcolm?" She whispered.

Wait, what?

"Clara?" I turned to look at her. She nodded and I pulled Maya into me as Anani stepped forward slightly.

"Who the hell are you?" My brother bit out in a low tone.

I knew that Maya said it was her father, well, technically. But this man had white blonde hair and blue eyes. He looked nothing like her and the anger on his face was one that had me growling.

"I'm her father," he smirked and then looked at her. "Her father, who had no idea where she was until he turned on the television. Come on girl, back to Louisiana with you."

I could see Clara bringing the children into the back craft room to make space for whatever the fuck this was. Maya shook her head and whispered, "Mother said you were dead."

"Your mother was a whore who took you from the safety of the church." he hissed out. "Look where you are now child, working and with two strange men. Plastered all over Hollywood like some cheap whore."

"They aren't strange," she murmured, looking nearly shocked and terrified. "I'm not going with you, father. I don't have to anymore."

"Like hell you don't," he growled.

"She's eighteen," I stated softly as his eyes sharpened.

"Do you have your birth certificate to prove that?" He grinned, showing off three gold teeth.

She swallowed, "The mating bond kicked into place, so I know I'm eighteen."

He froze, his jaw clenching, "You know?"

"You knew?!" She snarled, looking enraged as I shot off a text to Atlas and Croy nearby. Just in case.

"Of course I fucking knew," he snarled. "you are fundamental to our church."

"I'm not going back," she mumbled softly, her body trembling slightly. He stepped forward and she let out a small worried sound that made my brother step completely in front of her.

"Get out of my way, boy," her father demanded.

The door opened and I watched as Atlas and Croy both

took stock of the situation, noting how Maya's face was paper white.

Atlas looked down at him. "Who is this?"

"Her father," he snapped.

Croy let out a deep sound. "So one of the people who beat her?"

The man paled slightly. "We had to make sure..."

"You had to make sure of nothing," Atlas stated softly, "you have thirty seconds to turn around and get into your car."

His eyes searched them and pinned on Maya, "I'm not leaving town unless you're with me, girl, whether that is by force or willingly. Just remember that."

Then he was gone and Maya's body sunk against mine, her face icy. I watched as she mumbled to herself and watched him go. My much larger hands turned her small shoulders into me and she just seemed a bit defeated.

"Clara?" Anani called out.

"Go ahead!" The woman nodded, casting a worried look at Maya.

With ease, I picked her up and carried her towards the car, her head buried in my neck. I frowned feeling like something was terribly off. Like something about his words were true. I really didn't think he would let this go until Maya was back with him.

I wasn't about to let that fucking happen.

EPILOGUE - MAYA

My statement still stood true. Some people just didn't fit in in this world. I suppose it was a good thing I wasn't part of that world. I was part of something much more special.

Before experiencing this new world, I never believed that a singular moment could change everything. I assumed that life would be similar to living in the basement. Slow moving and monotonous. It had been a little over a week now though, Monday very late at night, and I sat in the darkness of the kitchen drinking tea and thinking about my father. One week and I had found out I wasn't human. I'd found an affection and connection I didn't think was possible. I'd removed the abusers from my life, all three, only to have one come back.

God. Seeing him had been torture.

I mean truly, it had been horrible. His face was as cruel as I remembered it and facing him, knowing the pain he was capable of, I'd froze up. Completely. I am not sure what would have happened if my mates hadn't been there. The twins seemed distressed. Atlas and Sai heated. Croy concerned and sleeping in my bedroom, waiting for me no doubt. Marco and Henry were in his office talking quietly about human legal constraints they could put on him.

I'm not sure it mattered.

My father was terrifying. More so than my mom in some ways because he, in his mind, hadn't been cruel with his beatings. No, in his mind, it had been 'God's mission'. Now that he admitted to knowing I was a shifter though? Things were coming into question. I needed to know more about the first seventeen years of my life, but I wasn't positive there was a way without asking him. Either that or I would have to go back and see for myself from my new perspective. Something I wasn't willing to risk.

"Angel?" Atlas asked quietly as two muscular arms came around either side of me.

Atlas. The protective and intense dragon had made me feel a sense of security since that first sleepover and still did. My body hummed as I leaned into him and looked up, those metallic eyes darkening slightly on my expression.

"You should be sleeping," he murmured.

"I know." I nodded and pressed my lips to his gently. He helped me up and wrapped his arms around me.

"Promise me something, Maya," he whispered.

"What's that?"

"Don't go anywhere by yourself for a bit, I don't trust him."

I grinned slightly, "Do I ever go anywhere by myself?"

Atlas chuckled and picked me up taking us towards the stairs. My eyes flickered past each half closed door as I considered the amazing men in my life. I snuggled closer to Atlas and a content, yet still concerned feeling flushed over me.

Croy was in my bedroom and as Atlas placed me on the

bed, the wolf tugged me forward. Atlas moved behind me and despite both of them being huge, I'd never felt more comfortable in my entire life. I closed my eyes, hoping to get some sleep. Anything.

"Goodnight, Sugar," Croy murmured.

"Goodnight," I whispered.

"We won't let him take you anywhere," Atlas reminded me and like it was somehow the magic words my body was looking for because I relaxed. Everything inside of me deflated and I closed my eyes. The thought that permeated before dropping into the abyss of dreams?

I hoped he could keep that promise.

I wasn't positive I could survive as I had, now that I know this type of love existed.

ALSO BY M. SINCLAIR

Vengeance Series

#graysguards

Book 1 - Savages

Book 2 - Lunatics

Book 3 - Monsters

Book 4 - Psychos (coming soon!)

The Red Masques Series

#vegasandherboys

Book 1 - Raven Blood

Book 2 - Ashes & Bones

Book 3 - Shadow Glass

Book 4 - Fire & Smoke

Book 5 - Dark King (coming soon!)

Tears of the Cosmos

#lorcanslovers

Book 1 - Horror of Your Heart

Book 2 - Broken House

Book 3 - Coming soon!

The Dead and Not So Dead

#narcshotties

Book 1 - Queen of the Dead

Book 2 - Tea Time with the Dead (coming soon!)

Descendant

#novasmages

Book 1 - Descendant of Chaos

Book 2 - Descendant of Blood

Book 3 - Descendant of Sin (coming soon!)

Standalone Novels

Peridot (Jewels Cafe Series)

The Grim Sisters

Forbidden Fairytales

Standalone Novels

Book 1 - Stolen Hood

Book 2 - Knights of Sin

FOLLOWING ME:

Link Tree: Link Tree
Email: MSinclairWrites@gmail.com

Made in the USA
Las Vegas, NV
13 February 2021